CROSS
PURPOSES

CROSS PURPOSES

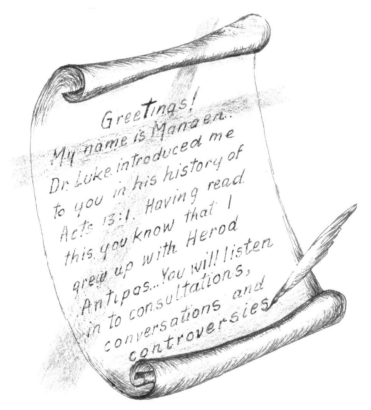

Greetings!
My name is Manaen.
Dr. Luke introduced me
to you in his history of
Acts 13:1. Having read
this you know that I
grew up with Herod
Antipas... You will listen
in to consultations,
conversations and
controversies

– MANAEN –
THE MEMOIRS OF A PALACE PEASANT

LUCILLE L. TURFREY

From Lucille

ISBN: Hardcover   978-1-6641-0028-2
               Softcover   978-1-6641-0027-5
               eBook   978-1-6641-0026-8

Cross Purposes is presented as a historical novel. *Major characters are actual persons.* The story includes a strong Biblical component to support the feasibility of the basically true story of 'Manaen who grew up with Herod' (See Acts 13:1).

All art, paraphrasing of Scripture, and poetry are by the author and therefore subject to copyright. Mavis Smith, friend and colleague over many years (and prior publications), has wielded her proof-reading skills once more to the benefit of this book and the author, for which I voice my thanks.

A disclaimer relating to the occasional Hebrew inserts is required: the author's knowledge of Hebrew is rudimentary though every effort has been made to ensure accuracy. It should be noted that vowel markings were not utilised until circa 7th to 10th centuries, A.D.

The author's research has relied on Young's Analytical Concordance, The Interlinear Bible (A.P.& A.), IVP, Beacon and Barclay Commentaries, Holman's Bible Handbook, The History of Christianity–A Lion Handbook, Josephus, and Encyclopedia Britannica.

Print information available on the last page.

Rev. date: 11/06/2020

To order additional copies of this book, contact:
Xlibris
AU TFN: 1 800 844 927 (Toll Free inside Australia)
AU Local: 0283 108 187 (+61 2 8310 8187 from outside Australia)
www.Xlibris.com.au
Orders@Xlibris.com.au
817258

CONTENTS

1. THE SHEPHERD'S FOLD

It was the season when lambs are born. Yehudith, my mother, had packed a basket of food and we had set off early to the fields near Bethlehem for Baruch, my father, was a shepherd. As I remember it, the mists of winter still clung to the hills. Clumps of snow lay round about. I wished the sun would take the ice away. There were new-born lambs just finding their feet, bleating for the ewes, needing to suckle, needing enough wool to be warm, then out with a bounce from the fold to the field.

Father cared for the sheep belonging to the temple priests. Pay was good and steady but the work was demanding. I doubted that I would be a shepherd when I grew up! These shepherds would stay out on the hillside day and night through the lambing season (they would need enough wool to be warm as well)! They had to be on hand to assist the birthing ewes. Much too cold for me! Why the shepherds were so faithful in their work I could not tell. The lambs would need to gambol about while they could. Their future would be brief! Those lambs were bred for sacrifice!

It was always good to be with my *abbi*, my father. Rough shod though he was, Baruch the shepherd was cultured in the *Torah*. The Law set down the rules for living. He was well aware that, while he remained out there on the hills of Bethlehem, he was deemed ritually "unclean". But we would go to him. I would be nurtured in the ways I loved. Sometimes, it bothered me. How was it really possible to live two lives all at one time?

Most times, I lived in the Herodion. In the palace, the décor was all opulence and elegance while dwelling in such decadence. With *abbi* and *emi*, my dad and mum, our small *bayith* (house), was humble but well-furnished by the warmth of love they showered on me. I knew where I would rather be. But Mother Yehudith's work was at the palace so there we stayed most times. Mother was the *yalad*, the midwife, and slave to the nursery. *Emi* (my mother), had raised the princes, princesses and one peasant—that was me.

We stayed out on the hills extra-long that day. While my father and mother caught up with the village and the palace news, I ran with lambs and ewes! It was a good day. I think of it now with joy—for the day and for the night and what it would bring into our lives.

The fields in which *abbi* and his men took care of rams, ewes and lambs are recorded, or so we're told, in the annals of our history. Here it was that Ruth, a maid from Moab, met Boaz, the "kinsman redeemer"— the one required to rescue a family member from bondage—of our Judah Clan! And who were they, you ask? They married and became the *abba* and *em* of Obed, the *abba* of Jesse! Yes! the *abba* of the "Shepherd King". King David roamed these hills when he was a lad like me!

The day was all but done by the time *emi* and I returned to the village. Too late now to trek up to the palace. We settled down for the night in our own *bayith*, located as it was just near the village inn. *Emi* kept the family home here for her help was often needed by the families of Bethlehem when babies were about to be born. Besides, she could share her life with Baruch, my father.

As I had not yet reached my strategic thirteenth year, it was our custom for me to stay close by *emi* until the actual date. Most times, we lived in the palace. There was plenty and more to be done by *emi's* work-worn hands.

It still amazes me that I, Manaen *ben*-Baruch, should dwell in the Herodion—the palace of King Herod. Not that I ever warmed to him. Didn't see him all that much. Throne rooms were not for the likes of me! Mind you, I would loiter by the massive doors at times. It was amazing to see just who would come to call on him. Oh yes! He was, most definitely, "The Great" one! Had the ear of Rome, he did. And foreign dignitaries would bow and scrape before the man. I did not like the king! I had my reasons and I'll tell of them, but first you'll want to know just something of the splendour of the palace perched atop the mount not far from Bethlehem.

The king was a master builder; in fact, the best! Look at the Temple if you don't believe me. After all, it's known as Herod's Temple—his name is as good as plastered on that massive edifice (why not the Signature of *YHVH*? I ask). And the name of Herod was as good as written large upon the great walls of the Herodion. This is the palace where King Herod dwelt for most of the year though, the Winter Palace down at the foot of the mountains near Jericho would lure him to escape into the warmth of the plains near the Salt Sea. There, the Jordan and the sea would cool his aching bones when he tired of his own massive pool. The king did not like the snows of Bethlehem!

When King Herod felt most vulnerable, he would flee the Herodion for Masada, his ultimate retreat situated on a high plateau by the shores of the Salt Sea. That sea was so salty it could be called "The Dead Sea". There were no fish in it!

The Herodion was most appropriate for the king—situated close to Jerusalem. That was a must for Herod, what with Rome requiring this and that from him. There it stands upon that cone-shaped mount which was raised to greater heights by the many workmen, making sure there would be sufficient space underground for the tunnelled water cisterns needed for this desert place!

More a fortress than a palace, it was dominated by four great towers that rose at least seven storeys high above the citadel. The Herodion appeared impregnable, certainly so when I was a lad! Look at the place! An outer wall no one could climb. No marauding bands intent on villainy would breach this fort. But inside, all was serenity, perfect symmetry—at least as far as stonework tells the story of the beauty of the place. Underneath serenity in Herod's home was turmoil, tyranny, intrigue and murderous brutality.

The palace was spectacular. Situated about seven miles south of Jerusalem and just over three, south-east of Bethlehem, the Herodion commanded the attention of all travellers near and far from home. It was built upon the desert's highest peak, Mount Hordus (it has been said that this was "the Mountain of the little Paradise"—it was not paradise to me. I'd rather be staying with *emi* and *abbi* in our little *bayith* in Bethlehem). But one could stand upon the ramparts and scan the far horizons. On a clear day, I could see Jerusalem! But, out there to the east and south, the desert lands reminded me that it was safer by far to stay within the walls of the Herodion!

It was my home—at least, my dwelling place. The formal halls of power were not inviting for a skid along the corridors! But I found time to peek into the awesome areas where Herod strolled to contemplate his plans and projects, his schemes and strategies. The king's residence was out of bounds for the likes of me but there was room enough to play and try a childhood prank or two. I always came off second-best!

The outer, fortress-walls were almost circular but, centrally, the palace was built more on the square. A grand staircase led down into the interior to the courtyards, the garden, the domed bath-house, banqueting hall and staff accommodation rooms.

At the very heart of things was the sanctuary—that is, the synagogue. Emi took me to the synagogue when possible. It was here I learned to pray. Here *YHVH El Shaddai* (the LORD God Almighty), became known to me. I was glad of that for here I learned the value of a peace not made by might nor power but that of inner *shalom* peace. As a boy, learning how to live an upright life in the Herodion when not truly 'at home' in our village *bayith*, my first steps into the Faith of my Fathers were made in the palace sanctuary, at my Mother's knee.

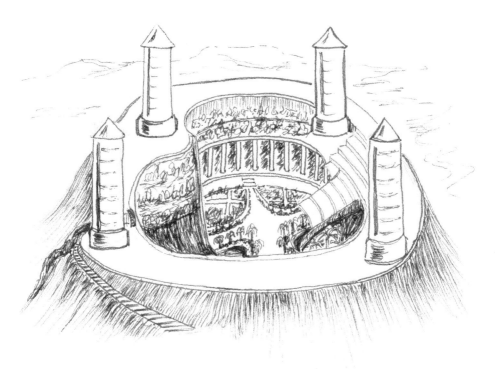

The garden was my special place. There was stately beauty all about. The date palms shed their fruit at times and I was very glad of that! There were palace paths where I could scamper round about.

And where, my favourite place? The swimming pool of course! I found a ready competitor in Prince Philip—he was more placid than the other princes, such as Antipas, and nearer my own age as well. I sometimes beat him as we swam across the palace pool. He did not like that very much so I tried to stay within the splashes of his heels!

It was rough and tumble in the playroom of the palace. The princes didn't seem to mind a rustle and a tussle with me. But I knew my place—they saw to that. There were no coronets in the playroom but airs and graces aplenty ensured my own subservience. That was us. "Yes sir, no sir, right away sir, if you wish sir," and when I chose to obey, we got on well enough most days.

2. NO ROOM! TAKE THE STABLE

The best of days was when I was able to stay awhile down in the village—like after the lambing season when *abbi* Baruch was able to spend a day or two at home with *emi* Yehudith and their lad, that's me, Manaen *ben* Baruch!

'*Emi, emi*, wake up, they are calling for the *yalad*. Come quickly to the door. The innkeeper is asking for your help!' Sleepy *em*! 'Watch the chair, the mat... We need some light.'

How well I remember everything. All that came to pass that night is embedded deep in my soul. Perhaps, at first, its importance was not realised so readily but now, in retrospect, I see it all with eyes made clear by faith! Let me take you there, back, far down that track of years:

• • • • • •

'Travellers, you say? The wife near her time? I'll come!' *Emi* takes me by the hand and, together, we go out into the night, following the innkeeper into the stables. The stables? Surely not! He explains that the inn is full but, when this couple staggered up to his front door requesting lodgings so late at night, what could he do? The host cannot turn the needy from a refuge in the night.

'This pair have travelled all the way from Nazareth, up in the hill country west of Galilee! It's beyond me that they ever made it thus far, the state she's in,' he comments. 'Had to come, of course. They belong down here for the current census of the Emperor Augustus—via Quirinius, Governor of Syria at the time—demands their signature! Anyone that belongs to the house and lineage of King David must find themselves in Bethlehem tonight! This is why, pardon my saying, the inn is over-full right now.'

The donkeys are restless. There's one all dusty and scraggy. He's munching hay fit to bust! Hungry beast. And the camels, wanting attention, unhappy with their lot. There are some oxen too. Oops, I've trodden in something messy there. This straw will clean it off. What a stinking stable this is!

The innkeeper hands his lantern over to the man who looks about to drop with weariness. Worry wrinkles line his face. He questions whether *emi* has the skill for such as what's about to happen here. He is assured for *emi* speaks of princes in the palace. This is enough for him. His shoulders seem to ease themselves! He takes me by my hand and leads me to a manger box. 'Now, my lad, you and I need to make a cradle from this box. Bring me some hay.' I spring to action right away.

The wife is wrestling with herself or what it is she fears, I think. An agony erupts and then, and then, the birth! I know how lambs are born out on the hills and it seems to me that another *kebes* (I like to have some fun with *kebes*: *kebaa-baa-baas*)—a new-born *lamb*— has just been born into a stable with a manger box to keep him safe tonight!

Emi places the "little lamb" into a manger, made soft and warm with hay, while attending to the needs of the mother there. I come right up to view the little son. He is awake. I touch his hand. I think I've never seen a hand so small as his. And the birth fluids are still upon him there.

He opens his eyes. I have been told that a baby at its birth will see not so much as its own mother's face! But this I tell you now: that little boy looks up at me; he smiles. I'm sure he smiles at me. And now, his little hand takes hold of the finger I offer for his touch. He takes my hand! '*Emi*, He took my hand! He smiled at me!'

'No, son. Not possible; it was just what you thought you saw and felt'. 'But, *emi*, he took my hand. He smiled at me!' This new-born boy would be my friend, much better far than princes who had never really smiled at me; their hands were only dragging, pulling, punching hands. I find no joy in princely hands. Perhaps this little boy could be, for me, much better than a prince! '*Emi*, what say, he and his *em* and *abba*, come to stay in the *bayith* next to us?' 'We'll see, my child.'

Emi takes the new-born baby, the "little *kebaa-baa-baas*" lamb, and wraps him up securely in the swaddling clothes made ready just for him. Everyone seems to be at peace now as the newest parents in the whole world find their rest upon the straw made ready for them on the stone floor. *Emi* turns to see her husband (yes, my *abbi*), staggering into the stable with his shepherd friends with whom we had shared that lunch, it seemed long ages ago.

Abbi's eyes are open wide. He barely looks at anyone except the "little lamb" asleep there in the hay! 'We've come to see the newborn baby!' 'How were you to know there'd been a birth tonight, with you away up in the hills?' *emi* asked. 'Yehudith, we have seen and heard what others wait a lifetime for and yet will never see!'

'You silly, darling man! You've seen a birth before and here's our "Little Man." to show for it!' 'Yehudith, what we've seen tonight, the prophets preached about!' 'Baruch! Do be sensible! The cold has got to you… Come, warm your hands, take a sip of wine the innkeeper has supplied for us.' He looks instead, to the mother and her new-born son.

'Beloved, there was a glory in the skies tonight!' 'Yes, we saw it too!' his friends now joining in the telling of the news. 'The angels sang to us! There we were, minding our sheep, looking for stray lambs, keeping wolves away, when the skies broke open! What we heard was wonder news. We were amazed, beyond all words to tell of it!'

'What was the message of their song?' *emi* asks with some humour in her voice.

Abbi wants *emi* to be sure that the wine was not speaking for him. He brings the conversation back to prophets and why they have a thing or two to say about tonight. 'What have prophets got to do with it?' I ask. 'My boy, I know the prophecies that count. You'll learn these words of holy writ as well before too long. Listen now to the supreme promise recorded in the prophet Micah's scroll:

ואתה ביתלהם אפרתה ... ממך לי יצא להיות מושל בישראל

And you, Bethlehem Ephratha ... out of you He shall come forth to Me to be Ruler in Israel. (Micah 5: 2).

'This prophecy, this word of Scripture so well known to us, tells us what has happened here tonight!'

The traveller, father of the new-born baby—Joseph, I discover, is his name—stirs. He sits alert, the tiredness gone. 'What's that, you say? Out of Bethlehem? So! that's why we're here!' What could he mean? He wakens his wife. 'Mary, listen to what these shepherds say. We're supposed to be in Bethlehem—not just to sign our names on Census Day. The reason for our trek down from the Galilee is for the birth to be right here! It's worth the journey now!'

The woman looks up. She smiles. Where do all those smiling faces get their joy? I wonder at what is happening in this stable tonight. The mother, Mary, rises now (with some pain, I think), and goes to the manger to take the little hand of her first-born son. There is a bonding of the two no one can interrupt.

Emi turns all serious now. 'Baruch! What did the *malakim*, the angels, sing? Was it a song we know?' 'Never heard a song the like of it before. Yet, Yehudith, it made such sense to us that here we are to see the boy!'

'But, Baruch, what did they sing? What did they say that brought you down out of the hills and away from the flocks to us?' 'It was a song of glory! Glory to *Elohim*, to God! Then, those messengers from God promised *shalom* peace, peace to people of goodwill!' 'Why, Baruch, why?' 'Because, my beloved one, a baby has been born in the City of David tonight who is the *Mashiach*—yes! the Messiah, the Anointed of God, to bring peace on Earth! They gave us a sign that what they sang to us was true. They said that we would find a baby lying in a manger. In a manger, Yehudith! And, there he is! This is *Yeshua,* the Messiah, he is to be the Saviour of the world!'

Abbi turns to the traveller, Joseph, to ask, 'What is the child's name?' Mary, the Mother, answers instead, beaming with such a happy smile, 'His name is *Yeshua*!' 'That little baby, *Yeshua, is* the One for whom we've waited all our years', Joseph exclaims and then he and Mary stand together at the manger beside their little boy. They know the truth of it. They tell their story then of visitations and the like in Nazareth, way up in the north, in the hill country just west of Galilee.

Mary, so young, hearing first-hand from an angel of the Lord, the astounding news that she would bear a son—the gift of the Holy Spirit breathing into her the Life of God. And Joseph, more mature in years, had been surprised by a dream where he was given instructions, by no less than an angel, to marry the girl for she was to bear a son who would be named *Yeshua* because he would save the people from their sins!

'You see,' Joseph said, 'this birth tonight in Bethlehem fulfils the prophecy of the greatest prophet of them all, Isaiah:

אות הנה העלמה הרה וילדת בן וקראת שמו עמנו אל

Behold, a sign: the virgin shall be with child and shall bring forth a son;
And she shall call his name 'Immanuel' (God with us).
Isaiah 7:14.

· · · · · ·

Two names then, that night for my 'little lamb': *Yeshua* the Saviour, who we now know as *Jesus*, and *Immanuel.* I thought of Joshua, the great warrior of our history. He had been true to his name. But *Immanuel*? How could *Elohim* really, actually, dwell with us. I would have to think

11

on that! Because of this little "lamb", God—*Elohim* Himself—would come to us, be with us! All this was more than I could understand when I was a little boy and besides, I was very, very tired. 'Good night *emi*, good night *abbi*. Goodnight everyone.'

3. THE PALACE GARDEN

It was a happy day. So seldom could I find a pleasant space of time when at the Herodion. The Princes, most of those boys older than myself, were prone to make the day a gloomy affair and I'm not referring to the clouds that sometimes clung to the hills of Bethlehem!

We sat together, chums chomping on the garden dates. The palms were laden and the fruit was ripe. *Maryam* (Miriam) was my friend. I cannot really say who was the mother of *Mimi* as she was known to me.

Not Queen Mariamne—the most predominant of Herod's queens—nor Malthace, who followed her into the king's bed, it's true but, you see, King Herod must have been the husband of at least ten wives. Those were the ones that I could count and, what of his harem there?

Mimi, Maryam, was about my age and she seemed to like my company. Just kids together; *Mimi* didn't use her princess power to make demands upon the son of her mother's *yalad* (midwife) and slave. *Mimi* felt secure in a friendship where her friend made no demands upon her time. She shared much of family matters with me. It seemed that Herod's brood had not so much to share among themselves.

I was told that Archelaus, Antipas and Philip were packing their bags. They were off to Rome to complete their studies there. I supposed this was a good thing for, if they were to learn about the power and policies of the Empire to which we all—including them—must bow and scrape, it was the place for them. It might be the makings of them. There was much I did not understand about the princes of Herodion! Their father was the king of the Jews. But Herod was no Jew! He had "alien" in his parentage. He hailed from Edom, was an Idumean!

Maryam spoke of her worries about the king. He didn't look so very well. The whispers were that Herod's days were numbered now. Where was there a space for sadness in my soul because of this? I had seen for myself the greying hair, bedraggled beard and worry lines upon the face. It seemed to me that Herod had no meat upon his bones in his latter days!

The Herodion was rife with jealousies, conspiracies and machinations of great intensity. How can I speak of it? I knew the source of the unrest and, if these records are to be complete, I must point to the king's residence. As I sometimes walked alone in the garden at night, the shrieks of pain, of peril, and the sounds of sorrow would penetrate the palace grounds. Pitiful moans, sudden screams, at times would pierce the shadows where I crouched to hide away from fear.

Morning gossip round the corridors would tell the wretched story of the night. Mariamne, the queen he loved most of all, it's said, was no more! A jealous rage had cast all reason to the winds. The queen was dead. Maryam had whispered, too, that three of her siblings were no more. 'Where are they now, Manaen? And what will become of me?' my *Mimi* asked. How could a boy like me find words that would encourage my young friend to hold her peace and hope for something better in the end?

King Herod's dramatic decline rendered him no longer rational. In the mind of those whose duty of care must have them tend his every complaint, belligerence and—towards the end—extremity of pain was surely, in some realistic ways, a payment for his crimes. Herod's disease would be the disease of men who could not control their lust, their abandonment of kindness or consideration for others or themselves!

Herod's final act of felony far outdid his palace treachery. The echoes of the village of Ramah's wretchedness are yet heard. At times, in retrospect, I find it hard to believe that even Herod The Great (the "great" what? Architect? Destroyer? Murderer?) could have stooped to such perfidy as to order the demise of hundreds of innocent children!

4. TETHERED CAMELS

Village life was like a holiday (indeed, a "holy day"). *Emi* and I were enjoying a period of rest at our *bayith* in Bethlehem—*Bayith-lehem*! How I chuckle even now at the name: Bethlehem, *the house of bread*. Indeed, it was. The bread that came from emi's oven was munchable all through the day. The aroma of fresh loaves upon the heated stone was like nothing else to ease the hunger and was so pleasant to taste. Father, Baruch, thought so too. He was always pleased when the lambing season was over. He could settle at night into village life once more.

Next door to us, the Nazareth family—whom we had grown to like so much—had made their home. Joseph busied himself with village carpentry. The events that claimed our attention at this time are such that I should take you back with me into the village scenes of the time.

• • • • • •

What I like most of all is to knock upon the door of our friends to find the toddler—yes, my *kebaa-baa-baas*, little "lamb", who loves to hold my hand. *Yeshua* (known as Jesus), is walking now. We sometimes wander up past the village inn, into the park and there to play awhile. He's always pointing to things of interest. He listens to the birds. He mimics them.

Yeshua will look into my eyes and he will smile at me. What's so new about that, I think. I know he likes to keep me company. There is a peace about this little boy for nothing seems to worry him. I wish that my life could be like his. One day, perhaps…

There's something happening in the village square. Travellers from afar, I see—their garb reveals that they have come from a distant country. I've seen robes such as these, at times, at the Herodion. These travellers are from a land far to the east, perhaps Iran or even Babylon. 'Come, *Yeshua*, let's find out where they are heading.'

The little toddler prances up and down with joy. Look at the camels. They are standing at his front door! He takes my hand again and leads, yes, leads me inside. The strangers appear to be awaiting his arrival. They are seated, at ease. As little *Yeshua* enters, the men rise. They bow to him. How like the visitors who bow before King Herod in his throne room at the Herodion! Jesus runs to his parents, Mary and Joseph.

Each man holds a gift in hand. In turn, they make their presentations to *Yeshua* who is the centre of attention. He is quite calm. There was gold—beautiful, shining gold—a powerful perfume (the name of which I learned was frankincense), and myrrh. Myrrh? Myrrh is a bitter herb. But this myrrh was an oil: known as "the oil of joy".

The first gift is meant to care for the practical needs of life; the second gift would aid the deepest thoughts and the third? Perhaps this gift might be meant to bring joy to the soul. I'm just a boy, I really do not know. These gifts could really bless one's life and ease one's death!

The visitors explain the purpose of their journey. Their story is incredible! They introduce themselves (I seem to remember names rather like, Casper, Balthazar and Melchoir). These men are known as "The Magi". They are astrologers, a priestly group whose studies focused on the night sky. They understand the movement of the stars. There's mysterious meaning in the skies and they can read the messages held in the stars, they say. The new, and brightest, star in all the skies had led them on their journey right from the east to the west. This was the reason for their presence here.

These travellers from fields afar had been to Herod's residence in Jerusalem—used occasionally when in conference with Roman officials. In requesting an audience with "the great one", they asked the perfectly logical question, 'Sire, where is the child who has been born to become the king of the Jews? We saw his star. It's a new star, the brightest star. It heralds the coming of a great king.'

The king seemed perturbed. We do not know why. He asked of us, 'When did this star appear?' 'Well over a year ago, your Majesty. We have been on the road ever since. There has been little time for holidays and holy days as the star has led us steadily on.' 'You've had a time of it, indeed! You will need some food and a good rest.'

King Herod arranged some accommodation and, next morning, he called us to the throne room. We think now that the king was finding time to discover the merits of our report. Is there something sinister in this man that we know not of? Indeed, while he seemed most placid in his words, we felt he challenged us.

'I think I know the reason why', Joseph, *abba* of *Yeshua*, breaks into the conversation. 'He would have summoned the priests and scribes in Jerusalem to ask just where the *Mashiach*, Messiah, was to be born. Their answer would, no doubt, have come partly from their knowledge of the *Torah*, though from a most unlikely source within it. The priests would speak of Balaam (who had a talking ass, the records say). He had been goaded into proclaiming, among many oracles:

קרוב דרך כוכב מיעקב וקם שבט מישראל
A star shall come forth out of Jacob and a sceptre
shall rise out of Israel. (Numbers 24:17).

'Then, Herod would be told the actual location from the wise men of Jerusalem—that which had been proclaimed by the prophet Micah.' Joseph then spoke the prophecy:

ואתה ביתלהם אפרתה ... ממך לי יצא לחיות מושל בישראל
And you, Bethlehem Ephratha ... out of you He shall
come forth to Me to be the ruler in Israel.
Micah 5:2.

17

This causes some consternation among the travellers, one explaining their dilemma. 'The king had said that he wanted to come to the place where we find the child so that he could also worship the Messiah. He requested a report after our visit here. We must think on this and decide on the route we must take for the return journey.'

The innkeeper has made the travellers safe for the night and, after a generous breakfast, the Magi make a hasty retreat with the explanation that one of them had been warned in a dream to bypass Jerusalem! I must check up on our friends next door to see how things are with *Yeshua*, the happy owner now of much gold and precious perfumes in those magnificent jars! He is not there! The family have gone! I run home to *emi* and *abbi*. '*Yeshua* has gone! His *em* and *abba* have gone! The rooms are empty!'

We hurry into our neighbour's *bayith* to find, indeed, no sign of our friends. *Emi* picks up a note of parchment. The departure is explained. It seems that dreams were seen aplenty in the night. Joseph had been instructed by an angel that he must take the mother and the child away from Bethlehem and leave no clue as to their destination. Would I ever hold the hand of my young *kebes*, "lamb", again?

• • • • • •

Why was it so imperative that those wise men, the astrologers, should receive such a dire warning in a dream that night? And Joseph too. They knew, in no uncertain terms, that they must depart in haste. They needed to be clear of Herod when he struck!

Herod was outwitted. This did not appeal to him! Repercussions were swift, horrific, and would mark the very worst of his atrocities! The edict was given that all boys of Bethlehem and surrounding districts, such as Ramah, who were two years of age and under—to be sure that all born from the time the star appeared were included—were to be slaughtered.

How deep the sorrows of those days; how wide the weeping, how great the grief. Blood flowed through the gutters under the feet of marauding soldiers throughout that sorrowful night.

Abbi Baruch brought to mind the words of the Prophet Jeremiah when news of the atrocity broke in on our humble home:

כה אמר יהוה קול ברמה נשמע נהי בכי תמרורים רחל מבכה
על–בניה מאנה להנחם על–בניה כי איננו

Thus says YHVH, a voice was heard in Ramah, wailing,
bitter weeping: Rachel, weeping for her children and she could
not be comforted… for they are not. (Jeremiah 31:14).

(Based on a statue at Yad Vashem, Jerusalem)

The last days of Herod gave part payment, at least, for the vicious atrocities that spilt the blood of innocents across the record of his crimes. It was said, by those who needed to remain up close by his tortured body that Herod's agony threw him into despair before death came to bring release—for him and for all!

5. SCHOOL DAYS

'*Abba*, may I join the rabbinic school?' It was the *shabbat* day of my coming of age. I was thirteen, no longer a child. I thought that I could call myself a man from that day on. It was early when I woke. I had no desire to waste a moment. What was the hope for that day and for the future life of Manaen *ben* Baruch? My active brain was already planning not just for the present, but for every future phase of life. I had become, at least according to our culture, a man that day!

Abbi, my dad, was a shepherd but he knew the *Torah* and lived by the tenets of The Law, as best a shepherd could. The basic requirements of the *Torah* were learned from early childhood at *emi's* knee. Now, the learnings of a child would not suffice for me. I needed to sit before the rabbis of Bethlehem to learn of Laws yet hidden from my eager mind. I wished to be a rabbi, I thought, when I grew to maturity.

On my special day, when all Jewish boys came of age, there was a celebration at our *bayith*. In rising from his seat at table, *abbi* intoned the famous quotation: *I thank You, YHVH, that I am no longer responsible for the sins of my son!* 'But, *abba*, I've been a good boy all my life. I do not enjoy the pranks of princes while at the Herodion! My *emi's* rules and yours, *abbi*, have kept me near the mark of what's expected of a boy.'

'*Beni*, my son, Baruch is my name and you have fulfilled its meaning in my life: I am truly the *blessed*! Manaen, in raising this glass to drink to your health on this, your special birth date, I can confirm that— when you were born—we gave you the special name "Manaen", a form of *Menuchah*, "comforter". You are more so, today! You quieten our souls! May *YHVH* bless our son: *May YHVH bless your coming in and going out from this time forth and even forever.*'

I'd shed the trappings of the child! The celebrations, going far into the night, sank deep within my memory. I was now deemed to be a "Son of The Law"! A family gift had been handed to me. With glee (much like that of a child, I must admit), I opened up my package to discover, joy! oh joy, a writing kit. Yes! More than all else, a writing kit would suit the needs of this "young man" whose aim was to become a rabbi, perhaps even a scribe. But first, I must be taught the ways of *YHVH* El Shaddai.

From that special *shabbat* day, I would be included as a trusted member of the required minimum number for our village synagogue to be in session. I could participate in every form of community life, bound to my *bayith* no more. I could lead the prayers in both the *bayith* and among the village families. I was a man!

I was still a growing lad, it's true, but new responsibilities were mine. The onus on blameless behaviour was now fully mine! The liability of choosing right from wrong was now wholly my decision. The need to heed The Law, the by-laws and the guidelines set down in ages past, must be known, must be met, must be displayed in every action of Manaen *ben* Baruch!

I made my private vow that day to honour *YHVH*, learn His ways, teach His values, all my life.

The question had been asked: '*Abba*, may I join the rabbinic school?' The answer was given. It had always been the intention of Yehudith and Baruch of Bethlehem that their only son should apply his brain and his soul to the study of The Law. 'Manaen, your name has been placed before the rabbis and they have agreed that you should start at once on your course. That you desire this to be so touches our hearts most deeply now!'

I found my seat in the room set aside for the rabbinic school in the precincts of the village synagogue. I had cast aside my palace life like an old suit of clothes, worn, ragged and soiled by many skirmishes among the princes in that superb but tainted "house of homage and horrors"!

There was a new dawn upon Bethlehem's hills. Its glow filtered down into the classroom where I set my writing kit upon my newly polished desk. My pen would record the many nuances that sat beside the actual Law of Moses that I yearned to emulate.

I felt a sudden squall of fear. How could I turn my mind to be precise in all the challenges to pre-conceived ideas presented in this class? The conundrums and the mysteries thrown at us lads by avid rabbis, keen to make of us the men we ought to be in sight of God and fellow man, should be enough to quell our quandaries.

But learn we did. The holy scrolls were opened to our eager gaze and the ancient script so revered by all, leapt out to challenge us, demand of us the path that we should tread to be worthy followers, students, "Sons of The Law". Come, sit awhile in class with me:

• • • • • •

'*Ben* Baruch! Read the text if you please.' 'Yes, Rabbi.' The sacred scroll is rolled back. The *Torah* opens to my gaze. I take the *yad*, the pointing stick (with that minutely carved hand upon its end to mark the reading place). Haltingly, I speak the words. I stammer at the magnitude of what the text conveys:

שמע ישראל יהוה אלחינו יהוה אחד
Hear, O Israel, the LORD, our God (is) One.
Deuteronomy 6:4.

'Now class, what is your considered response to this basic claim concerning the One we revere as *YHVH*?' 'We are to take heed, Rabbi; we are to listen.' 'Well said, Simeon; well said, but why should we take heed?' Benjamin takes his chance with the Rabbi: 'Because this is of utmost importance to our faith, Rabbi?' 'Benjamin, you have spoken better than you know!'

I have to speak my piece, huge questions rising ever higher in my mind. 'Rabbi, we read in the Holy Text that the Supreme Being has two names. He IS *YHVH*, He IS *Elohim*. Why is He known as *YHVH Elohim*?' 'Ben Baruch, your interminable questions begin to rankle me! Let the questioner answer his own question now!'

I struggle with my thoughts. *Moshe*, Moses, comes to mind. 'I think the starting place is Midian, beyond Ezion Geber.' 'You interest me, young Manaen; please, proceed.' 'Well, Rabbi, Moses had fled to Midian, as far as he could go away from his Egyptian foes. He was minding sheep.' 'Yes, what is so outstanding to your mind?' 'The bush that burned, Rabbi, the bush that burned. It didn't frizzle up. It stayed quite green!' 'We're all ears, young man, all ears!'

'Moses had to know the cause of how a bush could burn without a leaf falling to the ground. He marched right up to it. And, Rabbi, he heard the Voice of Heaven!' 'The facts, young man, the facts!' 'The Voice instructed him: *Pull off your sandals from your feet for where you are standing now is holy ground.* The holy scrolls record these facts.'

'Now then, Manaen, what are the words spoken there by the Most Holy One?' 'Rabbi, sir, He said: *I AM the God of your fathers, the God of Abraham, the God of Isaac, and the God of Jacob–Israel.*' I hide my face from the force of these words, just like Moses did that day in Midian.

'*Ben* Baruch, you have raised a question which points a finger at the Holy Personage. What is your problem, Manaen?'

It tumbles out before I can stem the tide of it. 'Rabbi, *YHVH* is the Great I AM. The LORD, our God, defies all limitations of time and space. He's just as much away up in Nazareth as He is right here. What is more: He IS with us, right here in this room. He IS at the creation of the world. And He IS at the burning bush! And, He IS with us when *Mashiach*, Messiah, comes. He IS, *Immanuel*!'

'And another thing, Rabbi. The One Most High is saying here that He IS the God of Abraham, He IS the God of Isaac, He IS the God of Jacob–Israel. Rabbi, does this not mean that Abraham, and Isaac, and Jacob, are now alive as well? He speaks the present tense, Rabbi. He IS the God of the living, not the dead. The text of Holy Writ has told us so!'

'You have put it well for a young lad, Manaen. Well, now, let us move on...' 'But, Rabbi, my problem is not with the Name *YHVH*, it is with *Elohim*. Why is God's Name—*Elohim*—so often written in the plural, sir?'

'Young man, you go too far; you try my patience with your probing and your problems with the Holy Writ! Plural? I'll give you plural! Explain to me the differences found in the very first statements of The *Torah*. The first: *In the beginning, created, Elohim, the heavens and the earth.* Then, the second: *And the ruach of Elohim was moving gently across the face of the waters.* So, young "rabbi", if you will: what do you make of that?'

I feel all eyes are on me now. I cannot, by lack of understanding or a want of faith in the veracity of *Torah*, denigrate the Holy Writ.

'There is a plural form that I see, Rabbi. The *ruach* cannot be *Elohim* yet it IS *Elohim* who was and IS—no, that is *YHVH*, I am confused—the Creator of the universe and all that in it IS! Rabbi, if *YHVH* truly IS, He IS *BEFORE* the foundation of the world! Yet *Elohim* is the Creator. But it IS *ruach*—the Holy Spirit—who appears to be the One that does the work! Rabbi, the Plural of *Elohim* makes Him ONE with *YHVH* and ONE with *ruach* just as well. 'And, Rabbi, what of the *Mashiach*, Messiah, when He comes. How will He fit in?'

'Quit while you're ahead, ben Baruch. Quit now! It's time for lunch.' We leave the room still munching on the mysteries being unrolled before our very eyes. But my questions remain unanswered. Will I ever know the truth of it?

· · · · · ·

Life had settled into some sense of normality in Bethlehem. Day time, rabbinic school; night time, happy respite with *emi* and, most times (when the rams and ewes and *kebes* allowed it to be so), *abbi* too. After the evening meal we would sit in the warmth of our *bayith* to share our findings of the day, our troubles and the pleasant things occurring to highlight the joys of family life.

Sometimes we spoke of those palace years and of the princely characters whose machinations coloured all the happenings at the Herodion. Favourite for *emi* was Queen Mariamne. As for me, my only friend was Princess Maryam who counted for little in the palace scheme of things.

The assassination of Mariamne will be forever held against the king—Mariamne, his one true love. Whether or not there was any truth in her disloyalty, one could hardly blame the queen. With her death, the magnificent dynasty of the Maccabees came to an untimely end. Mariamne was the last in the line of what became known as the

Hasmoneans, descending in more ways than one, taking the hereditary name from Hasmoneus, the forefather of Mattathias.

We would discuss the profound effect these warriors of old had upon this land. They had saved our nation from Antiochus *Epiphanes*, ("God Manifest"), the self-styled prince of pride who had plundered the Temple in Jerusalem. Judas—one of the five sons of Mattathias—proved to be a military genius. Known as "The Hammer", he was a wonder of a warrior indeed. Judas (mainly by surprise attacks), managed to outdo at least five Seleucid armies one after the other. His name remains legend throughout the land.

Politically, things had now changed irrevocably. Herod was dead. His sons had wrought their schemes and subterfuge to gain the throne. Archelaus and Antipas coveted the kingship. It would not be theirs. The one had gone to Rome to plead his cause and vow allegiance to the Emperor. The other, Antipas, plotted an overthrow and did his best to reverse the final decision.

Not long before his death, Herod had gone to Jericho, no doubt to rid himself of the consequences of his debauchery. The slaughter of the innocents of Bethlehem and neighbouring villages—over three thousand dead, I am told—was compounded by another felony of an entirely different ilk!

Herod had ordered that a golden eagle be placed upon the front entrance of the Temple in Jerusalem! After all, he'd said: 'It is my Temple. I planned it, had it built. I can do with it just what I want.

The eagle puts the finishing touch on this glorious building, dedicated, of course, to *YHVH*, LORD of Heaven and Earth! But it needs my signature. The golden eagle says it all!' All the golden eagle did was to confirm that Rome ruled the world, including Israel! The forces of Rome carried their 'golden' eagles on their standards and on their banners as their legions rode through numerous battles and countries to inevitable victory.

The consensus was that the golden eagle was a blasphemy! A frenzied mob, I'm told, stormed the gates and hacked the eagle from its roost! There were recriminations. Forty or more youths and their rabbis—Matthias and Judas—were taken, burned alive, slaughtered at the will of the enraged king who finally succumbed to the ravages of his volatile reign.

Herod had selected—after toing and froing on his choice as successor—the kindly looking, evil hearted Archelaus, but bowed to Rome for the imperial seal of approval. Archelaus won the day but not the throne. The Emperor 'crowned' him Ethnarch of Judea, Samaria and Idumea.

The vicious, black-hearted character of Archelaus boiled over when ranting, raving crowds refused to settle down. 'The killers of those youths must not go free!' 'We want a better High Priest!' 'Give us a High Priest who will care to keep the Ten Commandments, not the least of which is: *You must not kill!*' Stonings and worse ensued. Archelaus was incapable of calming the many mobs at large. He sent an army to quell the unrest. Many, many hundreds died. Caesar became perturbed! All this unrest could cause repercussions right to the very heart of the Roman Empire!

Rome had had enough of what appeared to Caesar as insurrection in that turbulent eastern corner of his realm. It must cease! Archelaus was deposed and banished to Gaul. He had ruled for just ten years. His jurisdiction ceased to be. Rome took control. The ethnarchy became the Roman Province of Judea.

'It appears to be the end of an era spanning almost two hundred years,' Abbi said. We thought then of Simon, Jonathan and Judas the three most prominent sons of Mattathias, who formed the dynasty known then as the Maccabees. Simon became the High Priest and Ruler of Judea and he was succeeded, in turn, by Hyrcanus, Aristobulus, Jannaeus, then Antigonus whose end was ignominious thanks to Mark Antony under orders, presumably, from Caesar.

My father made sure that his son would not be found wanting when it came to knowing of the comings and goings of the Priest–Princes of the Hasmonaean Dynasty. He tested me on names and places, battles, family trees, winners and losers in the power-plays of those times.

'Actually, *abbi*, the last of the Hasmonaean kings of Judea was Aristobulus II, whose mother was Salome Alexandra. Aristobulus II had defeated his brother Hyreanus II in a bloody battle.' Things came to an inglorious end when Pompey stepped in. Aristobulus II had struggled with the outcome but, for his disturbances, he found himself finally deposed and shunted off to Rome to eke out the rest of his days.

Pompey restored Hyreanus II as rightful ruler but under Roman control. He received assistance from Antipater, the *satrap* (a subordinate ruler), of Idumea. In turn, he was deposed then restored to his position by Julius Caesar who had by now defeated Pompey. Mark Antony appointed Antipater's two sons—Herod and Phasael—as *tetrarchs* ("quarter kings", I called them), of Judea.

Unbelievable crimes and cruelties eventuated. The Parthians were involved. Hyreanus' ears were cut off. This meant that he could no longer fulfil his responsibilities as High Priest. Herod had Hyreanus executed. Now he could flaunt himself as the singular Tetrarch of Judea. His power plays had just begun. I learned of his cruelty close up at the Herodion. How pleased, how thankful I was to be free of all the pomp and ceremony, yet devastating consequences.

Queen Mariamne—the grand-daughter of Aristobulus II—was, virtually, the last of the Hasmonaean Dynasty. She was, of them all, both to be applauded and pitied! I think I passed my test on heritage and parentage my father set for me.

It was during the final years of the Hasmonaean Dynasty that the two major sects of Judaism came into prominence. The more popular sect was that of the Pharisees—they were the scholars. The Sadducees were the aristocratic 'overlords' of the community. They were comprised of priests. Though smaller, I think, numerically, the Sadducees had surpassing influence.

What I remember from my youth was that the Pharisees were so numerous hardly a street corner could be found where a Pharisee was not holding forth on the qualities of life demanded by *YHVH*. They were the "High-n-Holies" as far as I was concerned. The Sadducees were adamant that rules and regulations were in order for the good of our society! They were, to me, the "Right-n-Righteous"!

The two other sects which held any significance in my youth were, first, the Zealots (just as well to stay quite clear of them if one wanted to keep the hair—and head—in place). The Essenes were "way out" in more ways than one. This strictest group of all lived in a very select commune down by the shores of the Salt Sea. They preached the sanctity of celibacy! They held great store by the Teacher of Righteousness. Spiritual enlightenment was their singular aim in life.

The Essenes valued greatly the many scrolls of Holy Writ they held in utmost security. Their life's work was to absorb, discern and declare the texts which brought Enlightenment.

Many throughout Judea and further afield were swayed by the ascetic ideals of this sect. However, devotees who lived a normal type of life in their own homes were not so strict in their observance of the convoluted intricacies of the rules by which this austere sect lived, and moved, and had their lives organised so rigidly.

My studies continued apace at Bethlehem's rabbinic school. I enjoyed the challenges by which the daily routines set by our rabbis aroused our spirited responses. I was not backward in coming forward, so to speak. If a matter scratched my brain, I would raise the issue with a longsuffering rabbi.

'Rabbi, what is the meaning of the rock?' 'Rock, lad? What rock has tripped you in your path to perfection?'

שמעו אלי רדפי צדק מבקשי יהוה הביטו צור—אל חצבתם

*Listen to Me, you who pursue righteousness, seekers of
YHVH, look to the rock from which you were cut...*
Isaiah 51:1.

'*Ben* Baruch, you are a "Son of The Law", you seek after personal holiness—you wish to be set apart to serve *YHVH* all your days, to pursue righteousness, to stand for right, denounce all wrong. Who is the 'father of your faith'? 'Abraham is the first of my fathers, Rabbi.' 'Young man, if you had journeyed further into the substance of that text, you would have found that, beside *the rock from which you were hewn*, is the *pit from which you were drawn'*. Never forget it, young man! Sarah stands beside her Abraham. Together, they have birthed Israel!'

The rabbi was wound up now. 'Abraham was the man confronted by *YHVH* to walk in His presence and live a wholesome life. Manaen, "Son of the Law", come view the text where the "father of the faithful" was called by the LORD to live a different style of life and to make a difference in this world! Observe what *YHVH* said to Abraham.'

The scroll was placed before me on the bench. I picked up the *yad* (hand) stick and began to read the precious words that became the imprimatur of all that would eventuate in the life of our nation. I realised that the words would have a profound effect on all my future days.

אני—אל שדי התהלך לקני והיה תמים

*I AM El Shaddai, (the Almighty God), walk
before My Face and be perfect (be whole).*
Genesis 17:1.

The scroll was sanctified to me! The text was new to me; the words meant LIFE to me! 'Rabbi, Rabbi! Look! Abraham was to walk in view of the FACE of *El Shaddai*. And I am to look to "the rock" from whence I was hewn. I am a child of Abraham. I, too, must walk before the FACE of *YHVH, El Shaddai*—the LORD, God, the Almighty One.'

I had not observed the entrance of the leading Rabbi of Bethlehem. He and his entourage were standing close by and, as he spoke, I turned to gaze upon "Headmaster". I was amazed. The Rabbi spoke directly to me. 'Manaen *ben* Baruch, your attention to the Holy Writ is exemplary. We, the teaching staff, have challenged you. But you have also challenged us! It has been determined that you will be no longer housed in the schoolroom of the Synagogue of Bethlehem!'

What had I done to deserve the disapproval of the Rabbis of Bethlehem? In what ways had I displeased these honest men? What will I do, cast off from all that I loved to do? What will become of me? I need not have feared. The "Headmaster" continued: 'It has been decided that you are to leave this hallowed, but elementary, school. You have been accepted into the premier rabbinic school in Israel. You will now become a rabbi-in-training at the Temple School in Jerusalem.'

The silence was deafening! I was stunned. But, after the first shock, everyone rushed at me in the ensuing excitement. It was astounding news. I must go home to *emi* and *abbi* to tell of it! What will they say? How will they cope with this, the day of my promotion to the Academy in Jerusalem? How will they react to my departure from Bethlehem?

6. "AT HOME" IN JERUSALEM

Jerusalem! Its gates have opened wide to me, the great wall that had been built so long ago, protecting it, the Roman Garrison fortifying it; the palace of Herod the Great and later, the occasional residence of Antipas, when required by Rome to be 'in town'; and the Temple eclipsing all else in grandeur. It would become my home (I had thought that I had seen the last of Herod and his handiwork)! But what a *bayith* for young Manaen *ben* Baruch!

I felt a piece of poetry forming in my mind. I must hurry to the writing kit (still my most precious possession), before these simple words will fail my memory. But first, to settle in. Where is my room? Where will I sit in class? Who will be the "Sons of The Law" that will be my fellow students? So many questions… I opened up my writing kit; some parchment was at hand! *(Source: Psalm 122:6).*

שלום שלום
"Shalom, Shalom"
The City cries—
Centre of Peace,
The soul's reprise.

ירושלם
Yeru-shalom:
City of Peace
Where seers have trod
Their souls to bare.

שאלו שלום
Shaalu, shalom:
A prayer, a plea
In Israel's heights
God's Peace to reign.

שלום שלוה
Peace and Prosperityw
May peace be found
Within your walls,
Your towers the scene
Of *YHVH's* vaults.

The songs of the Psalms are my joy. I do not keep rigidly to the patterns set down by King David and those who followed him in singing the songs of Zion (patterns such as agreement, antithesis and progression). I write to paraphrase one of David's Songs of Ascent because this is appropriate for me today as I have climbed Mount Zion on my first of days in Jerusalem, "The City of *Shalom: Yeru-shalom*".

LET US ASCEND

> Companions come,
> Let prayer ascend:
> For Israel's sake
> May peace attend.

> May peace now reign
> Within your walls,
> Secure shall be
> Your citadels.

> King David's throne
> For judgement stands
> And Israel loves
> The Law's commands.

> Let us now go
> To praise the LORD,
> His holy Name
> By all adored.

> Our feet shall stand
> Within your gate,
> Jerusalem
> Of wondrous fate.

> * Rejoice to hear
> The invite giv'n,
> Ascend to praise
> The LORD of Heaven.

(Psalm 122–Commence at *)

I search for the *shalom* peace of *Yeru-shalom* now as the sun has found the great Middle Sea! Would I ever see, would I ever sail on that great sea? It would take me to the edge of Earth. Or, would a ship just sail right on by to meet the sun upon another day? Impossible! Why do I think such things? Rest... Rest... That's what I need for a whole new world opens out to me when the sun turns up from the eastern sky to welcome the new day. That sun. It went down west. It comes up east. How? How, ever, can that be? Rest... Rest...

'*Shalom*. Good morning, class. All are ready to begin, I presume? Let me introduce a new student who joins the group this morning. Stand to your feet, Manaen *ben* Baruch, of the tribe of Judah—the princely clan. Give us to understand from whence you come and what will be your aims at Temple School.'

Not one moment had gone by without my rapt attention to the Temple Court, my entrance and placement in the class. Now I must speak for me! 'Rabbi, Bethlehem is my home village. I am *ben* (son) of Baruch, a shepherd on the Boaz Hills of Bethlehem. *Emi* is the *yalad*, (midwife) in the town. I have enjoyed my studies at the village synagogue since I reached the age of access as a "Son of the Law". It is my aim in life to be a rabbi, knowing The Law and the Prophetic Scrolls full well, sir.'

'Manaen *ben* Baruch, what of the Herodion? You do not speak of it.' I wished the question far from me. Yet, on this first of days, I must not question the Rabbi's intent, whatever it might be.

'I was but a child. It was a wonder of a place but, Sir, I knew my place. I played about with princes, saw King Herod at times, but mainly, Sir, I moved about with *emi* as she went on all her daily rounds. I've lived in the village since King Herod died.' I hoped that was enough. The rabbi let it be. I sat down at my desk and opened up my writing kit, my precious writing kit. But there was a stirring and a murmuring in the room. I felt all eyes on me. Please, let me be, I thought.

'So, *ben* Baruch, you played with princes when a child and you, a peasant lad! Let it be said on this, the first day of your life with us, you are a prince, young man! You are as a "lion" of the Tribe of Judah, the princely clan. Let it never be forgotten, whatever will become of you, that—from your birth—you've been a prince! Allow the "peasant prince" his place among us in our Temple School! Greetings, Manaen *ben* Baruch, you are welcome here!' My life at Temple school had now begun. I would come to know Rabbi Judah *ben* Judah very well!

'Our current studies find us immersed in the scroll of the prophet Isaiah. What do you know of Isaiah–son of *Amoz* (the strong)—during the reigns of four great kings, *ben* Baruch?' 'Rabbi, he was the *PRINCE* of prophets, Sir!' Laughter broke out. I retreated to my shell. Hardly the way to start my course.

'Class, fill us in.' The chorus chimed in: 'Must have been born nearly eight hundred years ago.' 'He knew the kings and the high priests very well.' 'Rabbi, he as good as lived in the Temple.' 'He was a married man, Sir.' 'Well, then, Simeon, his sons; he had two sons. The meanings placed upon those names, young man.' 'The one means *a remnant shall return*; the younger son's name means something like *hurry to the prey*, Rabbi.'

I'm itching to ask about the *remnant*, who comprise the 'remnant'? But not today—I've said enough already today. The discussions continued, much to my delight. So many new truths leapt out at me as the scroll remained the centre of our attention.

'Who is the *Mashiach*? What does Isaiah say? What clues has he given as to the identity of "The Promised One"?' 'Yes sir, I know, sir. I know the names,' Ethan called out, it seemed to all and sundry in his excitement. 'Speak out the names then, Ethan!'

יועץ	פלא	אל גבור	עד–אבי	שר–שלום
Wonderful	*Counsellor*	*Mighty God*	*Everlasting Father*	*Prince of Peace*

(Isaiah 9:6)

'Reading now as for a list, how does this translation assist us, class? We will hear your thoughts!'

Wonderful Counsellor:	'He understands our worries and our woes, Sir.'
Mighty God:	'He is *El Shaddai*, Oh, same but different: *Gibbor*.' 'He is the Warrior who will conquer all, Rabbi.'
Everlasting Father:	'He has no beginning nor end, Rabbi. He is *YHVH*, the I AM: past, present and future.'
Prince of Peace:	'He is, well, He will bring *shalom* peace to all, Sir.'

Here is my "plural problem" all over again and… and… something deeper, more mysterious. Up goes my hand. 'Rabbi, *Mashiach* is singular. He is one person yet Isaiah assigns to him the plural name of *Elohim*, in his list given the title *El Gibbor*, (the Mighty God). There seems to be a "trinity" of names yet He is ONE God—the *Torah* tells us so! And, Rabbi, sir, I do not understand how the *Everlasting Father* can be the Son—the *Prince of Peace*.'

'*Ben* Baruch, the name *Prince of Peace* speaks of youth, vitality: the *Everlasting Father* brings His peace to us with vitality! *YHVH* does not age!' But Rabbi Judah *ben* Judah had not answered my question. Would I ever find an answer? Is there an answer?

The rabbi, no doubt, felt that it was best to move on. He addressed the class at large: 'What do you consider to be the turning point in the life of Isaiah?' One of the senior pupils responded with, 'It was the year that king Uzziah died, Rabbi. Isaiah was in the Temple when he heard a choir the like of which was never in that Holy Place! Then Rabbi, he saw—he saw *YHVH* … in the Temple Sir! It must have been a magnificent sight, the whole Temple was filled with the Presence of *YHVH*, LORD!'

'What was the outcome of this vision, lads?' Again, the choatused response: 'He SAW the glory of God!' 'He REALISED that he was unclean.' 'He HEARD the angels sing!' 'He RESPONDED by confessing his faults, sir.' 'He CONFIRMED his commitment, Rabbi.' 'He was CHANGED, Sir—he was sanctified. From then on, he lived a holy life.' 'Well said, class, well said.'

'Isaiah revealed much about the Character of *YHVH*, *Elohim*. Some facets, please, gentlemen.' 'LORD of Hosts.' 'The Mighty One of Israel.' 'Isaiah says that He is the Redeemer of Israel, Rabbi.' 'He is the Holy, Holy, Holy … why three times said, Rabbi?' 'Just to bring an emphasis, young lad, to bring an emphasis.' I did so much want to question him about a "trinity" of holiness. But, not today!

'You interrupt my train of thought. Now, where was I? What are the main messages that you may find imbedded in this Holy Scroll?' '*YHVH* wants us to know that He cares for us.' 'He understands our problems and our sorrows and that He is the healer of our pain.' 'He is like a shepherd to us all; He will feed us, He will lead us ...' That was the point of the whole discussion for me. I had to speak:

'He gathers the young, tender lambs in His arms, holding them close to His heart and gently leads the mother ewes. (Isaiah 40:11).

Rabbi, is the Good Shepherd the same Shepherd as the One of whom the prophet Ezekiel speaks?

I will raise up one Shepherd over them—My servant, David—and He shall care for them. I AM the LORD who will be their God and My servant, David, will be a Prince among them. [He shall feed them and He shall be to them a Shepherd]. (Ezekiel 34:23).

'May I ask, Sir, how can Ezekiel have spoken in the future tense so many years after the life and death of David, King of Israel? I know he was a shepherd lad, Rabbi, for he shepherded his father's flocks out on the Boaz Hills near Bethlehem. But he is dead and gone these many years. Is there another "David" who is yet to come who will be the "Good Shepherd" of Israel? Will the *Mashiach*, the Messiah, become the "Good Shepherd" of all Israel, Rabbi?' The Rabbi cut me short. Perhaps it was for the best on this my first of days!

'*Ben* Baruch, you get ahead of yourself. All in good time, young man, all in good time.' (But the Rabbi failed to answer my question). 'This class is done for the day. Take note of the project required from each of you. It should be completed before *Shabbat*. As you are well aware, Isaiah is the present focus of our studies' (settling his gaze on me). 'Memorise the words of the scroll's prophecy on *The Joy of the Redeemed.*

'The purpose of this project is to bring emphasis to a major feature of the written work of "the prince of prophets" (*cough, humorous cough*). *Ben* Baruch, you are to paraphrase this important section, using the same genre utilised by Isaiah. We will discuss your findings when we meet in next week's Isaiah class. Dismissed!'

I would need to stay close by the Temple Scroll. It was not familiar yet to me. *The Joy of the Redeemed* … Oh yes, I do remember now. I asked a scribe to roll back the scroll to the place where it begins:

ישׁשׂום מדבר וציה ותגל ערבה ותפרח
The wilderness and the dry land shall rejoice;
the desert shall exalt as it blooms.
Isaiah 35:1.

I am to take up these words, absorb the power of them, and turn them into phrases that will mean the same but come wholly from my brain? *Eloi,* my God, give aid to me! I read on, then over, all the words again. The patient scribe stood by my side (no doubt to guard the precious scroll). I would come back to the scroll tomorrow to confirm that what I am about to set down in the words already forming in my mind will suffice. I returned to my assigned room within the precincts of the Temple Courts, all thought of food gone from my mind… *Hallelujah!* My poem was finished before the *sabbath.*

'Manaen *ben* Baruch, the word from Bethlehem informs us that you've been known to write a poem or two. Read, if you please, the poem you paraphrased from the sacred text!' The fear returned. How would these words, reconstructed from the Holy Writ, stand up to the test now laid on me? I stood … began …

THE JOY OF THE REDEEMED
From the Isaiah Scroll

This barren wilderness, vast plain of arid waste wind-carved:
This crimson sunburnt land, bleached branch, and stubborn root, rain-starved,
Will dance once more for celebrants will stomp the ochred dust
Displaying ancient sagas, memories of deeds long past.

For drifters in the desert lands of life, health-harmed and wan,
There is renewal—welcome rain on sun-parched sand—hard won.

39

Now activate those halting hands, make straight those quaking knees,
For faith's firm grip steals ground from fear as Elohim responds to pleas.

When the Mashiach appears, we'll see the Light, our thoughts made new;
The lame will dance, the dumb will sing as springs surge through.
Streams deep and wide will flow where blossoms' fertile seed abides
And reeds will grace with life the rim of welcome, quenching tides.

This is God's country and His Highway leads through our abode
Of sand dune, rugged rock, and gulch cleft deep. This is the "Road
Of Wholeness and of Holiness"; no evil beasts will strut, untamed, upon
This holy ground, but ransomed souls shall walk the sacred path unharmed.

Redeemed—released—restored—renewed: hand-held and courage found,
The "New Day" dawns! God's love pervades as Freedom Psalms resound.
His Kingdom comes—a vast unmeasured, timeless, sin-swept land:
No more required are sorrow's tears as joy and peace descend.
(Isaiah 35, paraphrased)

I sat, exhausted in my seat. What did the rabbis think of it? How had they tested it as I read down my screed? There was silence in the room. Then, someone clapped his hands. Other hands joined in. It seems all were applauding me. But what would the rabbis say?

'*Ben* Baruch, you have caught the joy that is in Isaiah's Psalm! I must point out, however, that your work has extended somewhat over the more precise treatment of the original. Isaiah is more explicit in the language of his song. I might say of your work that it is more in the way of a *prolonged* paraphrase. And I think that you have lived in desert lands for far too long!

'We cannot accept the incessant rhyming of your poem. The Psalmists did not fall into such patterns in their songs! But young man, you have caught the gist of the poem. That, and better, will do!'

A lad I had not met before sidled up to me after the morning class had broken up and rushed off to the midday meal. 'Manaen, your poem was just what I needed to hear. I found myself rejoicing in how you emphasised the major truth concealed in Isaiah's wonder-work! My name is Johanan, by the way. You may call me Joh.'

'What do you think Isaiah was compelled to reveal, Johanan?' 'The One long promised, the One for whom we search. *Mashiach* will come and He will right the wrongs that tarnish all the land!' 'Yes, I feel it deep within my soul. I'm glad that you also believe! We'll compare our notes when possible. It's good to know you, Johanan, Joh. Let's go to lunch!'

When we arrived, it was difficult to find a space to sit and eat. There was a buzz of excited chatter in the meal room. A finger or two pointed in my direction. I hoped the conversations were not derogatory! There was a smile here and there, a frown or two to balance out the thrust of noonday gossip! This too will pass, I thought.

There was a stir of expectancy when next we met together to study the Isaiah scroll. We wondered what would be the focus of discussion as the scroll was opened to our gaze.

The rabbi spoke. 'We continue with "the prince of prophets", you will be pleased to know! The course curriculum requires a comprehension of the structure of Isaiah's scroll. The charcoal will allow a listing on the wall for all to scrutinise. Where do we begin?' 'At the beginning, Rabbi?' The rabbi took the comment in his stride but turned upon the lad with a stern reply. 'Commence at the beginning, Samuel!'

With his head a little bent and looking towards the floor, Samuel shuffled to the writing wall and wrote these words for all to see:

חזון ישעיהו
(The vision of Isaiah)
and followed it with:

משלים ודברים
(Parables and Oracles)

'Well done, Samuel. The introductory section is complete! What will come next? Who comes to place some charcoal on the wall?' A student responds, comes forward with reticence to print:

יהוה בההיכל
(YHVH in the Temple)
Another student wrote:
ימנואל
(Immanuel)

'The section is, basically, complete. And we will move on. Nathan, come, receive the coal.' The student wrote:

תושבים
(Foreigners)

'That will suffice. We will move on to the next portion of the Scroll. Manaen, step forward now.' I came to the wall. Took the coal and wrote:

משפט וגאלה
(Judgement and Redemption)

Rabbi Judah *ben* Judah smiled benignly at me. 'Do stay at the wall, *ben* Baruch. Set down a title for the next portion upon the wall.' I turn again to the task, pressed hard upon the charcoal and wrote:

אוי וזהר רבות
(Woe and warning multiplied)

Reasonable, "Son of The Law", but your grammar is somewhat stilted!' I return to my seat chastised. 'Next, if you please, Joseph.'

החדש נשף
(The New Dawn)

'That will do nicely for "*The Joy of the Redeemed*", Joseph. Please, continue.' Joseph reclaimed the coal and wrote his thoughts:

אמונה וירא
(Faithfulness and Fear)

'Excellent, Joseph. You have captured the essence of the faith of Isaiah and the fear of King Hezekiah during that turbulent period. Take your seat. Class, we have—until now—been studiously investigating the first half, more or less, of the Holy Scroll of Isaiah. We have come to a strategic movement in His style of prophecy. What is the great change that takes place in his prophecies?' He looks at me. I'd already guessed it would be me to find the title of "the second half" of the Isaiah scroll. I speak the word in answer to the rabbi's question and he throws to me the black charcoal. I move to the wall and write the words:

ישועה
(Salvation)

There is a twinkle in Rabbi's eye! He's pleased with me. 'In just one word, *ben* Baruch, you have encapsulated the whole! Salvation is, indeed the crux and burden of the whole. However, the introduction to the final section of the scroll is the word *Comfort*. We find comfort in salvation! I ask of you, *ben* Baruch, a Psalm that will paraphrase what you consider to be the paramount text of Isaiah's timeless masterpiece.'

I knew at once the actual text to contemplate that I might set down a worthy chant. It must be done before *sabbath*. Just two days hence our class will consider and review my work. I hurry to my room to start the printing of the words that have carried such deep quandaries in my mind. How strange that the chant was formed so seamlessly. It was ready for the scrutiny of the rabbis and my student company on time.

THE SUFFERING SERVANT

Who has believed our word,
To whom is God made known?
Grown like a root from driest ground,

43

No majesty is shown.
Despised, rejected, sad,
We all had passed Him by,
But He has borne our many griefs,
Was smitten, left to die!

The Suffering Servant, pierced;
Was crushed for what we've done!
He carried sin to bring us peace.
Through death, He did atone.
All we like sheep have strayed,
We turned from Him away!
But God has laid upon His soul
All our iniquity.

He silent came to death,
Like unto lambs, was slain;
His tomb aligned with wickedness
Though He had done no sin.
Yet, after death, comes life,
His soul is satisfied!
Because through death he bore our sins,
Our soul is justified!

Therefore, He is assigned
His portion as the Just,
Rejoicing in His victory
Because His death sufficed!
He bore our sin and shame;
For our transgressions, slain.
Accounted as the sinner, blamed,
He did not die in vain!
(Isaiah 53. Choir: *Chalvey* C.M.)

The stark pain expressed in Isaiah's psalm pierced my heart. A tear fell on my parchment, quickly smudged away. The rabbi did not speak. The class was silent. Then, Johanan spoke. 'How is it possible, Rabbi, for a person to be *assigned* the greatest portion—I suppose—in Heaven, if the one of whom Manaen has written looks nothing better than a dried up root in desert sands?' 'Yes, Rabbi,' another raised his hand, 'The man in the poem is despised, he is rejected, and sorrowful. Where and how did he pick up my griefs to carry them instead of me having to carry my own burden myself?'

'Rabbi, the One promised by Isaiah doesn't sound very much like the *Mashiach*! He was tortured; he was pierced; he was crushed; he died and, Sir, what does that word "atone" mean?' 'Yes, Rabbi, how could he make things right by dying? That sounds very much like defeat!' 'To answer the prior question regarding the word "atone"—and therefore also your own, young man—I need to point out that this is a conglomerate word meaning to make at-one, to bring together, to reconcile. The *Messiah* will bring us, together, home to God!'

Another student then cut in. 'The one bit about it that I can believe is that we are all like sheep, like silly sheep, wandering sheep, out there roaming on the hills, not knowing how to find our way home to the fold!' 'Rabbi, how can I be justified if *Mashiach* is, hmm, vilified?' Another asked, 'Rabbi, it was *Elohim* that placed the burden on his soul. How could God put anybody's iniquity—all the iniquity—on the soul of *Mashiach*?' The rabbi, finally, rose. '*Ben* Baruch, you wrote the psalm, answer Nathan. What have you to say for your psalm?'

Now I felt every eye in the room burning into my back. For some unaccountable reason, I thought of sheep; the Boaz Hills of Bethlehem. Yes! that's it. Boaz, "the kinsman redeemer" who was willing to give up all for the sake of Ruth! I gave my answer then: 'It is because *Mashiach* is The Kinsman Redeemer, Sir! He is willing to give all that we may be released from sin!'

'Interesting supposition, *ben* Baruch. This gives you all something to think about as you go to lunch.' The class stirred, eager to leave the room. '*Ben* Baruch, stay. I wish to speak with you.' 'This is it!' the rabbi will have my hide for such outspokenness!'

'*Ben* Baruch, Manaen, you reveal a tenacity in your studies that is most commendable. I value your input in relation to the identity of the "Kinsman Redeemer". It is a supposition worth pursuing. However, there are aspects of your contribution to discussions that need some honing, clarifying, if you will. It has been decided to assign to you a mentor rabbi who will be able to guide you in the paths set down in the Holy Script. Your mentor's name is Nicodemus. You may have met him. Nicodemus has just graduated from the Rabbinic School. Young, yes, but competent, a valued member of the team. You will find his expertise to be already noteworthy.

'One more thing, *ben* Baruch. As yet, you have not qualified in terms of written work. Your psalms are lacking in essential structuring. I've set some homework to which you must respond with alacrity and certainty.'

I was handed a parchment that carried just a heading though enough to know what was required: "AN *aleph beth* PSALM".

Johanan—my new friend, Joh—was beckoning. 'Manaen, "My Man", over here. I've kept a seat where we can chat while chewing on the meal. Are you all right? You were called up to hear what Rabbi Judah *ben* Judah had to say about your "performance" in class this morning. Were you attacked? Pummelled? Expelled?' I guess I looked to be in a daze. Well, I was, but not for the reasons Joh reckoned as my woes.

'Thanks for keeping a seat for me, Joh. And no, I think I'm still in one piece—just!' 'What happened in there? You look all done in!' 'I have to write another psalm. And, this time, I am to obey the rules of writing. The rabbi has requested an acrostic psalm—entirely my own work. That is, I can't rely on the precious scrolls of King David and the like.

'I'll help you, Manaen. I've been at it for longer than you have. I think I have a decent grasp of what's required.' 'Sorry, Joh, as much as I'm in need of it, your help cannot be given. It is a lone assignment and I must prove my understanding of the Holy Writ!

'By the way, something else. I've been assigned a mentor. Seems I cannot reach the mark that is required without some help. My so-called "tutor" is to be Rabbi Nicodemus, just graduated from the school. Perhaps Nicodemus can help me come up to the mark the rabbis demand of me.' 'But, "My Man", that is no gauge! This is a sign that you have given the rabbis hope that you'll amount to something great!'

'How do you know?' 'Ah ha! You see, I've been given a rabbi mentor too!' 'You have? Nicodemus?' 'No, another teacher just graduated along with him. His name is Gamaliel. I'm wondering what he's really like. I hear that Gamaliel is intent on joining up with the Pharisees and that he is really a Pharisee, a Sadducee and a zealot, all rolled up into one. Heaven help us, Manaen. Let's not join any of their parties. Let's join our own! Come, let's feed our face; we'll miss out on lunch if we don't hurry now.' We sat for some time, when food was done, mulling over matters that related to the feeding of the soul. 'Joh, I have to go. My homework is yelling out at me.' I sped to my private 'den' and began to write:

AN *aleph beth* PSALM
for

YESTERDAY	TODAY	TOMORROW
Confirmation	Thanksgiving	Hopefulness

א	*aleph*	First and **foremost**, You are *Elohim*, Eternal God; I honour and adore Your Holy Name.
ב	*beth*	LORD, You are my Refuge and my Sanctuary. I find my one true **home** in You.
ג	*gimel*	You lead me on the mountains, in deep valleys and in arid desert lands; I do not fear my **pilgrimage**.

ד	*daleth*	The **door** You open, *YHVH*, leads to abundant life; in going out I find my joy and, coming in, my rest.
ה	*he*	You **windows** open out to vistas glorious; Your wondrous grace is always in my view.
ו	*vav*	O LORD, I am secure when **held** by You; Your loving-kindness never fails; I will not fall.
ז	*zayin*	In You is **Life**; O *Elohim*, You give me strength; I grow in knowledge of Your will from day to day.
ח	*cheth*	LORD, You "**companion**" me, I find You near; You walk with me, reveal my way through life.
ט	*teth*	When **evil** threatens, I will look to You for help; in goodness and in kindness You will tend my soul.
י	*yodh*	You hold my **hand**, I am secure: You care for me; I am Your child, You reach right down to me.
כ	*kaph*	In Your **open hand** is all I need; in body, mind and soul I am replete.
ל	*lamed*	You have **instructed** me in all the way that I should go; Your discipline encourages me to be upright.
מ	*mem*	You are the LORD of turbulent and troubled **seas**; when I am terrified, You calm the storm for me.
נ	*nun*	You **challenge** me to face my fears; I'll take the route You mark for me.
ס	*samekh*	O LORD, You will **support** and strengthen me; rough country is made smooth by Your own help.
ע	*ayin*	My **eyes** are focused on the LORD and where You lead, I follow on.

פ	*pe*	I am to walk before the **Face** of *Elohim*; it is the LORD who makes me whole.
צ	*tsadhe*	From before my birth, O LORD, You have **nurtured** me; as I follow Your decrees, my life will be enhanced.
ק	*qoph*	All Your commands are **sure**, there is no uncertainty! You issue Your decrees with powerful emphasis.
ר	*resh*	My **mind** is stayed on *Elohim*, my God; You do instruct me how to choose the right.
ש	*shin*	The LORD is my shield, my refuge; You are my **guard**; My safety is assured as I rely on You to guide.
ת	*tav*	I know my great **Redeemer**: You have set me free; You offer me Your life that I may have true life!

I shared my work with Johanan who became quite reticent to offer a response to my first, I hoped, truly Hebrew poem. I could not see the fault of it so took it with me for my interview with Rabbi Judah *ben* Judah. He listened attentively and made no comment till I came to *tav*.

'Manaen, my lad, I pat you on the back! I see that you agree at last to conform to the time-honoured patterns of Hebrew poetry. I see that you have kept within the framework of an acrostic poem assiduously. Also, to my surprise, you have employed the well-defined "agreement" style effectively, though you have vacillated, grammatically, between 2nd and 3rd person at given points within the psalm.

'However, Manaen, I am amazed that you have managed to capture the hidden meanings in each letter of the alphabet. I wonder how you managed that! You have, in fact, produced a set of "picture parables".

'So far, so good. But, *ben* Baruch, you have failed to knit the key acrostic words with their following commentaries sufficiently. In fact, there is no unity at all beyond the thoughts provoked by the pictures you have managed to draw from our sacred language. However, from whence comes such an astute rendering of the hidden truths suggested by your verbal illustrations, lad?'

How could I answer such a probing question? And did I know the source of a knowledge that has now been actually disclosed to me? I do remember that, back in Bethlehem, a rabbi had shown to me a more ancient form of Hebrew lettering. Those early "scratches" were really nothing more than pictures which indicated the sounds to be uttered. Yes! that's where I came to know the lines and shapes that gave to me these "picture parables". I explained this to Rabbi Judah *ben* Judah.

The rabbi acknowledged that, indeed, the most ancient form of Hebrew, discarded around five hundred years ago, set down the messages of The Law and The Prophets quite pictorially. 'After all, *ben* Baruch, one picture is worth many, many words!' He then went on to say that I would need to learn the methods of the scribes so that I could become proficient in the art of melding words into a cohesive whole. I needed to gain the ability to present my work in the shape of an ideal manuscript that could be presented in assembly! 'Come, Manaen, meet your tutor, the Rabbi Nicodemus. He will make of you what you can become!'

'Rabbi, it is my one desire to seek after truth!' He turned to me, looked deep into my eyes. '*Ben* Baruch, do not go searching after Truth. The Truth will come to you.' I wonder what he meant?

I found Nicodemus to be a man tall in stature and in character! Somewhat reserved, it's true, but in his quiet demeanour—surprisingly—I found a confidence that all would be well with us! There seems to be a kindred spirit in our approach to the demands of the rabbinic school. He was not at odds with me. I found support for many of my emerging views but, when a wayward thought exposed itself, Nicodemus would quietly put me to the rights of it. I liked the man!

The Isaiah course was all but complete. I did rejoice that this final section of his massive work—the history, the prophecy, the poetry— would centre on a future time for which we yearned with varying degrees of expectancy. As for myself, I devoured the content of those final prophecies bound up in the poetic masterpiece of the Holy Scroll.

Just think a while! Imagine all the chatter that exploded in our class as we spoke of such wonders as:

Arise, get up! Be all aglow for your Light—the glory of the LORD—rises upon you. His Light will dispel the deep darkness! His glory will appear. How bright that Light! The nations of the world will flock to you!

The Spirit of the LORD—the King—is upon His Anointed who will have the responsibility to preach Good News to the deprived, the broken-hearted, the captives. He will announce the Day of the LORD!

One day, the righteousness of Zion will be made known. It will shine just as a new day dawns. Your salvation shall be likened to a great beacon. You shall be known by a new name!

Here comes one clothed in red garments. He has trampled the winepress alone. He will tell of the kindness of YHVH who, in His love and mercy, redeems them… (Why, O LORD do we wander)?

Oh, that You would cleave the skies and come down to us. Since ancient times none has perceived, no one has heard nor seen any God like You for You come to the aid of all who follow You with joy in their heart.

The LORD was found by those who did not call to Him, to nations that did not call upon His name. He revealed Himself: 'Here am I, I have opened My hands, My arms, to you but you have not listened.

The LORD declares: 'Heaven is My throne and the Earth is My footstool. Where is My House? I will esteem those who are humble and truly sorry for their sin.

Discussions on these major themes engaged our minds and much was learned from the greater texts surrounding the selected quotations

I have paraphrased. That final day of the course set out for us on "the prince of prophets" would prove to be a major highlight of our studies for Isaiah does not complete his work before declaring:

This is what the LORD says: I will extend peace like a river…
I will comfort you just as a mother will her child…
You will rejoice when you see this happen…
YHVH's hand will be revealed… He will execute judgement upon sin…
All nations, all languages, will come to see the glory of YHVH…
Those in distant islands who have never heard of Me will tell of Me.

It was *YHVH* who had the final word—He pronounced the "benediction" on the Scroll of Isaiah:

In the same way as the new Heavens and the new Earth that I create will endure always, so will your name, and your descendants, remain always!

What a fitting conclusion. Our chattering and clattering continued long after Rabbi Judah *ben* Judah had rolled the scroll on Isaiah.

'*Ben* Baruch, come by my desk, it's time we reviewed your work regarding the Isaiah scroll.' 'Yes, Nicodemus; I'm just collecting my writing tools.' Should I address him as "rabbi"? I wondered. He didn't seem to mind the more informal nature of our association. Perhaps, I'd better ask. 'No, Manaen, that's not required by me. You recognise that my role is to walk with you through your studies. I do not expect a disrespect! So, let things be just as they are.

'Tell me, what have the climactic themes of Isaiah's prophecies brought into that astute young mind of yours?' I found it easy to open up to Nicodemus and, generally, he put to peace the thoughts that troubled me.

'*The Light will shine on us*! Light brings sight! One day, we will see all that *YHVH* has in store for us!' 'But, Manaen, we will have need to face the Light. Otherwise, we will find ourselves in a deeper darkness. When one turns from the Light, how deep that darkness! But do go on.'

'The Mashiach, the Anointed One, is preparing to come among us.
How wonderful, Nicodemus, the Messiah will focus his attention on
those that are heart-broken and those in bondage. I am surprised!' 'But,
why surprised, young man? Unless the captives are set free, we'll all be
in bondage—to Rome, yes, but also to our sins! What next have you?'

'We will be known by a new name! Nicodemus, what could that new
name be?' 'Consider this: the name will relate to the *Mashiach*. What
is the meaning of his name?' *'The Anointed*, sir.' 'You are beginning
to be fluent in the *lingua franca* of our time—Greek. How will you
translate his title in the Greek?' 'Well, let me see… That would have
to be *Christ*, sir.' 'Correct, young man. Though at this stage I cannot
begin to understand how "*Christ*-ian" could correlate with *Mashiach*!'

'The garments of the Coming One will be stained in red. I have a
fear upon me now that those stains may not be caused by grape juice,
Nicodemus.' 'Then, Manaen, what is the red you fear?' 'It's blood,
precious blood, Nicodemus! But then I find the Holy Script declaring:

*'YHVH will come to the aid of any one who follows in His path with
joy.'* 'Where do you envisage that path to lead?' 'Nicodemus, the path
will be narrow, it will lead uphill and down in the depths as well, like all
paths of life! It will be a stony path but "walkable" because the LORD
will guide us in that very path.' 'We're coming up to the last full stop.
What next?'

*'The LORD makes Himself available to alien nations, those who do
not know Him. He will open His hands to them.'* 'So, Manaen, why does
not humankind listen to the Voice of *YHVH*?' 'I think that too many
things crowd out the possibility of listening to the LORD. The din is
too loud. There is no "silent place" where we can hear His voice.' 'May
you continue to "listen" well, Manaen. And, finally?'

*'The LORD declares that Heaven is His throne but Earth is where
He will plant His feet. He asks, 'Where is My home?'* 'Where, just where
is *YHVH's* home?' 'His home is in my heart, Nicodemus. It is in my
heart!' 'You've said it well, my young friend. Come, let us go to lunch.'

7. ANCIENT ALLEYWAYS

The sun was warm upon my back. It was early afternoon and there was no homework set for me. We had completed our studies on the Prophet Isaiah (although my personal application to the challenges frequenting his epic work would stay with me, needle me, rankle me, encourage me, guide me on the path I had chosen). Nothing pressing would impede a leisurely stroll through the ancient streets of the great city. There was no purpose in the stroll other than to become more familiar with the streets and alleyways, the homes of the high-born and the low-born too. By now, I knew the environs of the Temple quite well but there were quarters of the city yet unknown to me. I was on my way to acclimatise myself more fully with the character of "David's City".

MANAEN'S CITY OF JERUSALEM

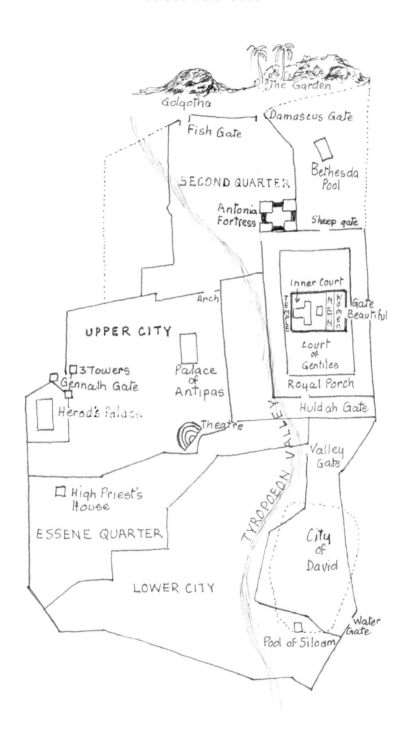

I exited the Temple Courts via the Huldah Gate and wandered southward into the Lower City. Turning then, I made my way westward into the Essene Quarter. I stood awhile to take in the surprising splendour of the High Priest's house, situated quite near to the access gate into the Upper City. Should I venture any further? Curiosity gained the better of a wiser mind! There it was, still one of the major attractions of Jerusalem: the City Palace of Herod the Great! I thanked God that there had been no necessity to ever lay my head upon an ornate pillow in that "home of history"—the good and the grotesque!

A courtier (whom I recognised by his mode of dress) stood by and I questioned him as to the towers dominating the palace. 'Well, sir, that tower is named the "Tower of Hippicus"; there, to the right. Then, there's Phasael's Tower hard up against the outer wall. And the nearer tower is that of the Queen—Mariamne. We are quite glad of that tower, sir. It helps to keep the memory of the queen still in our mind.'

I thanked the man then turned eastward, heading towards the Temple grounds. But there, before any thought of returning to my living quarters, I saw it then: the Palace of Herod Antipas! I'd better beat a quick retreat. But… but… who is this? A young woman, dressed in the finery that revealed the high position of the "vision of beauty" now approaching me. Her jewellery flashed in the lowering sun. A princess, this must be. But surely not. It cannot be…

I saw a look of wonder in her eyes. She stared at me, a question unspoken, yet quite evident. Then, 'Manaen? Is it really you?' 'Maryam! It *is* you! I thought it too good to be true!' '*Manni*, I had heard from friends that you are studying at the Temple's rabbinic school. I'd hoped to find you…' I stood before her, silent, a wonder in my heart! 'Oh, Maryam, *Mimi*, it's really you. I've found you again. I've been lonely for our walking and talking in the palace grounds of the Herodion.' Her smile matched mine.

'Come, walk with me. Where are the places that I may meet with you when my studies will permit it to be so? How free are you to share a stroll with me, show me the city sites and, well, just sit awhile and chat like we used to do? How may I contact you?'

Questions tumbled out unchecked. Happy answers came in response. How quickly time will fly away when an hour seems like a moment of our time. We did find time enough to stroll a while and neither minded that the hands were held. 'Manaen, there is a place that I love to frequent. It is a garden, not like the palace garden at the Herodion, but it is a special place. It is found beyond the city's northern wall. Come with me to find the place where we can meet.'

I had not thought to find a scene so tranquil—in sunlight, quite magnificent. This would make a lovely meeting place. But there, just west of the garden was a hill—more like a mound, in fact. How could a hill appear so starkly horrible, rising up to spoil this beauteous place? I pointed out the mound to Maryam. 'That is *Golgotha*—Skull Hill.'

I saw what she meant. How very like a skull. Its hollowed "eye" caverns and its fiendish, glaring grin were comprised of rocks gouged out by time to form the unmistakeable leer. 'Look, Maryam, those would-be eye sockets appear to be caverns.' 'It is said by many that here may be found the grotto of Jeremiah,' Maryam replied.

Jeremiah? I was about to study the life and work of this great prophet of the past. Perhaps a cavern could become my private place of study when I needed to escape the noisy hubbub of the rabbinic school! 'Maryam, in spite of the features of "The Skull", there is something about this place that intrigues me, calls me back again.'

'I think that "Jeremiah's Grotto" could become a place of personal reflection. I may come to understand just why Jeremiah said the things he said and bore the pains of "The Weeping Prophet" the way he did. But, dear friend, the day has sped away from us. I'll walk you home. We'll meet together in the garden one week from today!'

For the first time since my coming to Jerusalem, I felt that I had "come home"! But what a balancing act I would need to keep in place. Study, obviously, must be paramount. But I had found Maryam, *Mimi*. I must never lose her again! Unchartered yearnings were astir in me!

8. INTERROGATION AT THE TEMPLE

It was somewhat disconcerting to find that Rabbi Judah *ben* Judah had been replaced and the rabbi in charge of the Jeremiah course is to be Rabbi Joseph *ben* Jamin. A venerable man, the rabbi's age— we hoped—would provide for us a profound depth and width of understanding that…

'Come quick! You cannot miss it. It is amazing. Quite bizarre! A boy! Look at him there, among that heap of rabbis.' Johanan tugged my cloak and we hurried on to where a crowd was gathering but, surprisingly, there was a stunned silence abroad. There, in the Temple Court of Men, was a sturdy young lad yet not "of age". Around the boy were seated some of the finest rabbis of our school. Yes! There was Rabbi Judah *ben* Judah… Nicodemus, I see there too. Joh and I edged closer until we could hear the exchanges taking place.

I could not understand this dramatic scene! How could a mere boy command the attention of the Temple's intellectual elite? What's that he asks of them? Where did a question such as that come from? The boy spoke with a northern accent, hardly conducive to a serious debate. His clothing was simple, home-spun. Bronzed by the summer suns, this lad had no need of clothing that would mark him out as the son of a celebrity, or a cultured voice displaying his tutoring by learned men. He held "the floor"! (Well, the courtyard, actually).

What's that he asked? All search around for some men of studious intent to give an adequate response. None came. Another question to challenge the teachers: '*YHVH*, according to the Holy Writ, IS the God of Abraham, the God of Isaac, and of Jacob. Gentlemen, this honoured text is set in the present tense. It has been thought, without a qualm, that Abraham, Isaac and Jacob also, *were* all dead. How come, the present tense?'

Oh, joy of Heaven! My question asked again. What will the rabbis say? But, not a word? The rabbis fail to answer it! Another question is now flung at them: 'King David wrote a psalm that commences with…' (This child knows the Holy Scripture, knows it well! How come, such knowledge from those despised northern climes?) 'But, let me first ask, who is the *Mashiach*?' An answer now: good old Joseph *ben* Jamin! 'Why, the son of David, of course!'

'Then why, Rabbi, did King David record these words, '*The LORD says to my Lord: sit at My right hand until I make Your enemies a footstool for Your feet*'? Please, tell me now, if the *Mashiach*, Messiah, is indeed "the son of David", why does David refer to him as "Lord"?' Silence reigned!

Joy! Oh joy! Outsmarted by a boy. Unforgettable! It would be almost twenty years before I would hear that question again. And then—as now—there would be no answers, just an ever-deepening hatred for… But I get ahead of myself. I also had some questions to be answered, of a very different kind.

Who was this child? I stared at him. He returned my gaze. He smiled at me. He smiled at me! Where had I seen that smile? No! No! No! Surely not! But, that smile?! The boy left the stunned rabbis and the gathered onlookers. He came right up to me. He took my hand!

Kebaa-baa-baas? Kebes? My little "lamb"? '*Yeshua*, is it really you? You are alive?' There was no need of a reply for he smiled at me! I wanted, then, to hug the boy. But a pandemonium broke out. A woman had broken through to the Court of Men! An older man was at her side, endeavouring to restrain her. "My son! *Yeshua*, my son! How could you do this to us? A day out, on the road to Nazareth. We couldn't find you. Returned to the city. We've been searching for three days! Three days, *Yeshua*! How could you have done this to us?'

'Mother, *emi*, dear; do you not know that I must be doing what my Father asks of me?' His father? But surely, here was his father, intent on chastising his—supposedly—wayward son! Yes! this was indeed Mary and Joseph whom I had liked so much back there, those years ago in Bethlehem. They were not dead! They were alive. The family had escaped the slaughter of Herod's murderous rage. I was so sorry that Yehudith and Baruch, my parents, had already returned to Bethlehem following the Feast of Passover. They would have been ecstatic at such a reunion. I would send word to them!

Joseph, tired and overwrought, took his child's hand—a little roughly, I thought. But still, they had been searching for him three days… In the streets and alleyways of Jerusalem! For *three* whole days: Lost! No wonder they were perplexed! *Yeshua* waved at me. He said, 'I'll find you again one day!'

The class began. Rabbi Joseph *ben* Jamin introduced himself (as if he needed to). 'Today we begin the saga of one of our nation's most revered prophets, Jeremiah. Class, the meaning of his name, if you please!' We knew it well but Samuel spoke up: 'It means, *YHVH is exalted high*, Rabbi.' 'Should not a more appropriate name be assigned to him, gentlemen? Why not, for example, "The Weeping Prophet"? Not one of us could offer up a worthy reply. We knew, full well, the dire events surrounding the great man of our history, long past. It was enough to make him weep; there was no doubt of that!

'Before too many days, gentlemen, I will expect a worthy response to this, my initial challenge to you all. Be assured, it will not be the last of the questions with which you will be faced. But, in the introductory discussion found within his work, can any tell me who are the two engaged in conversation as his story does begin?' Not one of us would venture a reply. The scroll was yet to be unrolled in our class. Two senior men approached the rabbi's desk. They held the sacred scroll so carefully. It was unrolled.

'Nathan, come, take up the *yad* and begin to read.' The *yad*, the hand-held stick (so that he may not touch, despoil, the holy scroll), now firmly held, Nathan began the sacred story of Jeremiah:

ויהי דבר–יהוה אלי לאמר הלך וקראת באזני ירושלם
And the word of YHVH came to me, saying:
'Go and cry in the ears of Jerusalem…
(Jeremiah 2:1).

'*Go and cry?* Why, the tears, Nathan? Why, the tears?' 'Because Jeremiah was "The Weeping Prophet", Rabbi?' 'We may need a new title for Jeremiah, gentlemen! But first, the time zone that is the focus of our study now?' There were some ready responses at last. 'It was in the days of Josiah, *ben* of Amon, king of Judah, Sir.' 'Followed by?' 'By Jehoiakim, *ben* of Josiah, Rabbi.' 'Then?' 'Zedekiah, also *ben* of Josiah. He had a sorry end, Rabbi, a terrible end!' 'My son, the king was not the only inhabitant of Jerusalem to suffer so appallingly in the days of the history now before our eyes and mind put to the task; I trust, also, within your heart and soul.' I warmed to him. But, not for long.

'The opening reports that are left to us from Jeremiah's history is couched in poetic terms. As you are the "resident poet" in our midst I am informed, *ben* Baruch, I lay on you the burden to produce, before *sabbath*, a poem—I ask of you in classic Hebrew style—to set us on our way. Perhaps you will inform us, in your work, of a new title for the prophet we will survey!' Rabbi Joseph *ben* Jamin, I thought, had cast a cynical eye on me. It challenged me. It worried me. It rankled me. I'll give to him a poem he would not wish to see!

It was our meeting day—Maryam and me. My mind had strayed already. Perhaps, I had misread the intent in the aged eyes of my new teacher of the Law and Prophets, so to speak. When the class had concluded its conversations and controversies, I made my way northward through the Damascus Gate. And there, I feasted my eyes upon that garden laid out so near to the city walls. It was early. Maryam would not come to me for at least an hour. I chose to walk over to *Golgotha*, climb into the grotto I had assigned as the most likely site where Jeremiah, oft times I was sure, had found a refuge for meditation, contemplation and—yes—discussions with *YHVH*!

My mulling over the task in hand took me back, down through the centuries, through histories sunk deep within the psyche of our people. Sometimes, true and faithful servants of *YHVH*; most often times, Israel chose to be in rank rebellion against the disciplines "imposed" upon a sovereign people surely free enough to choose their own specific aims and gains. So very often, they—that is, we—were a people bent on pursuing foreign paths of plenty, and with them, alien gods that took their fancy. They bowed to wood, they bowed to stone!

How could our ancestors consider wood and stone to be our "saviours" from the foreigners that set about smashing down our gates and walls… aliens who brought their gods with them? Will we ever be a people who could learn the lessons of our past? What could our past inform us concerning these present times? What could we learn from the past today? The Law and the Prophets speak to us! What will they say to my class down there in the Rabbinic School?

The heat had not as yet left the day but I was shaded here from the worst of it. From my vantage point, I could gaze out upon the City of Shalom to find my peace. I'd find some peace, I knew, in the good company of Maryam. But here, before me were the ancient city walls the masterful towers, the many "Herod" buildings dominated by— over there, towards the east—the towering Temple (Herod's Temple, Solomon's long gone). To the west: the triple towers associated with the palace of Herod the "Great"!

I opened up my writing kit. A little battered now from so much use. My precious writing kit! The poems, the psalms it had produced; and still it challenged me to open up some fresh parchment to respond to this latest assignment that must emerge from the point of my writing tool! Where do I begin? … Here is "Jeremiah". *YHVH* comes right down to him, enters in this grotto sanctuary. The great *I AM* disclosed His presence, here, within this ancient grotto now sanctified unto the LORD once more... The poem began to flow:

JEREMIAH
HIS CALLING AND COMMISSION

O Jeremiah, Jeremiah! You are the son of Hilkiah:
when Josiah ruled, I came to you. You heard Me call
your name—well-chosen name: 'YHVH is exalted' is your name.
Before I placed you in the womb, I knew you well! I saw, in you,
an aptitude—before your birth—that you'd fulfil My plans for you:
before you breathed, set quite apart to prophesy, to preach with worth.

But, LORD, I'm but a child! I do not have the skill to speak with clarity what You desire of me; I do not have the means within my soul to prophesy, make known a doom so dire.

You must not see yourself just as a child for I have chosen you
to speak for Me: I will direct you where to go and what to say.
Don't be afraid of enemies for I'll protect you through
your life. Through sorrow, you will find true worth!

The sovereign LORD then reached to me,
He touched my lips and said to me:

Now you've received the news that I command you'll give:
you are appointed to proclaim that—for sin—there's no excuse.
What do you see upon your watch, O Jeremiah: say?

I see a branch of almond tree! It's winter, LORD, but this
tree sprouts before the spring arrives.

So does My word come quickly! Let the nations know I hasten to
fulfil My word. Consider more: what do you see now, Jeremiah?

I see a boiling caldron, LORD; it's tilted from the northern clime!

You have observed My news: it's from the north that fire will come,
engulf the land, destroy each home. The eastern kings will come,
despoil the Promised Land throughout Judah. It's then My people will
be judged, condemned. Get ready to stand firm: proclaim My word!
And, Jeremiah: Know that I AM with you. I'll see you through
these times!

I sat awhile, considering the words that lay upon my parchment now. What terrifying news that youth—Jeremiah—was saddled with!

If Jeremiah held within his soul any sense of sorrow, despair, horror, for what he'd heard, he'd find the tears quite readily. Oh, yes, Jeremiah was "The Weeping Prophet" right enough. In setting down the poem upon this parchment now, I felt the tears as well. After all, it was the Promised Land about to be engulfed. I love this land! How could our people have brought things to such a sad demise? I wept for it, my land. 'LORD, spare our land today!'

But wait! The last word! The last… promise? I re-read the words still drying on the parchment:

Jeremiah! Know that I AM with you; I will see you through these times!

That's it! That's it! Jeremiah is *NOT* "The Weeping Prophet"! He is "The Prophet of the Promise"! No, no, not that… I've got it now! Jeremiah is "The Prophet of Hope"! I wonder what our sage rabbi will say to that?!

Oh no! I hear the ram's horn! The time! The time! What will Maryam be thinking? Not far… Not far… There she is! Maryam waves her welcoming hand to me. She comes to meet me. Now, there's a *"spray of almond blossom"*! Should I *"hasten my words—should my words come quickly"* to convey what is in my heart for her? It cannot be! Maryam belongs in the palace—be it belonging to her brother, Herod Antipas— and I am but a peasant. What can I offer her?

'Manaen, I thought that you'd been held up in rabbinic school… that you had forgotten…' 'Say no more, dear heart, er, my friend! The homework held me back. But I have finished it. Let us walk together in our garden now. Look, there, the almond blossom is bursting from its buds. Spring will soon be here. What are your plans for spring, Maryam?' 'That does depend on… Oh, Manaen, what does the future hold for us?'

Is this *"the branch of almond blossom"* for my yearning soul? I paused. Maryam waited, a question in her eyes. 'Maryam, I see no springtime for my heart. I am a peasant, I can bring no gift to you, the princess of my heart' (there, I've said it now). 'Your future is mapped out for you. And mine is too. There are different paths ahead for us.'

'*Manni*, I have no wish to entertain the foreign princes and satraps that Antipas is prone to fling at me. I have no wish for palace drapes; these jewels are a weight on me that I'd rather cast aside if I can stay by you. You are the 'jewel' that I'd wear with pride!'

I think that I had gone beyond the words to frame my thoughts. I looked more deeply in those lovely eyes—they had been the first of Maryam to captivate my mind, my heart. But reason had to rule.

'Maryam, *Mimi*, my dear one, let us take a pause on what we feel, what we'd like to promise now. There's "blossom" on the breeze; perhaps, for us, a springtime like none else! But pause awhile, consider what you'd lose. And I must think about just how I'd give to you all that you would deserve!'

'I'll wait, but not for long, Manaen. I know what's in my mind, my heart! Perhaps it's best I talk with Antipas. On his better days, he can give thought to weighty things. I'll seek the time most opportune. When next we meet, Manaen: will it be winter or the spring for us?' The question remained unanswered. '*Manni*, I care not for these sudden showers. Please, take me home.'

There was a buzz of anticipation as Rabbi Joseph *ben* Jamin shuffled towards the speaking desk. The Jeremiah scroll had already been opened up for scrutiny. The rabbi eyed his students, scanned the class, found my worried frown. '*Ben* Baruch, your homework: present it to the class. Everyone, give your attention to the resident poet, please. Be ready to respond with some detailed analysis.'

It seemed appropriate that I should move up near the desk. I opened up my parchment with its poetic paraphrase as requested. I began to read, *Oh Jeremiah, Jeremiah! You are ...* The lines went on, and on. Did I really think to write these words in just that way? Did not the LORD, Himself, encourage me as I had sat, almost certainly, in the grotto of Jeremiah. It was his sanctuary. And it had become mine!

'My young Manaen: you have the makings of a Biblical scholar! Well put. You have introduced the rudiments of that initial conversation between the youthful Jeremiah and *YHVH* with surprising prowess. Is he still to be "The Weeping Prophet" *ben* Baruch?' Would I now be putting my foot in the murky mire once more?

'Rabbi, while there is ample reason for the title usually assigned to him, I have a new thought now. In spite of all the negatives, the dire warnings that Jeremiah would have to prophesy about: at the end of his first conversation with *YHVH*, Jeremiah receives a wonderful promise. It is a promise that I believe sustained him throughout his drastic circumstance during that gruesome period of our history.' 'Don't be so convoluted with your verbiage! First, the promise, *ben* Baruch, the promise, if you please!'

'Well, Sir, after *YHVH's* warning that His people would be judged and condemned, then comes the challenge for him to stand his ground. *YHVH* says, *Jeremiah, know that I AM with you now.* That is the promise which kept Jeremiah as the LORD's own man throughout all the traumas that would befall him and the nation. That promise gave him hope, Sir! Jeremiah is "The Prophet of Hope".' The room erupted in controversy. Those for my supposition heaped praise and those against, condemned the title in no uncertain terms! One new student, a young lad but vocal above the rest, could not accept such a preposterous statement. There was no consensus at the lesson's end.

When I met with Nicodemus for his estimate of what had been presented to the class, I made so bold as to ask who was that volatile young man with such a foreign accent. 'He is from the Diaspora, Manaen. Tarsus, I believe. Oh yes, Saul of Tarsus. I fear we will hear much from him! He will be tutored by Rabbi Gamaliel, I hear.'

The class leant every which way when next we met. That new title, given so tentatively by myself, had set everyone in a twist! Rabbi Joseph had seen the likes of us for so many years past, he knew the wiles with which to draw us into a more disciplined framework on which to pursue the course.

'Today, gentlemen, we will look at the pros and cons! What will steer our thoughts to hopefulness? Is it possible to discover "The Prophet of Hope" in the text before us now?' 'Never, Rabbi, never! There was no hope for *shalom* peace in Jeremiah's day!' 'Let us determine the strength or weakness of your argument. Gentlemen, I put you to the test. Line up two lists: The Problems and the Promises.'

The work began with much toing and froing round the class but, gradually, the charcoal markings filled the wall with the lists reflecting our diatribe. Students took it in their turns, it seemed to me, to use the charcoal on the wall. Slowly, the lists took shape. I found it a remarkable way in which to test our knowledge of the prophet's recording of events that were in those days, yet to take place. It helped us, also, to remember vital evidence of what was once, to many, sheer speculation!

PROBLEMS	PROMISES
Israel had defiled the Land	*Israel had been guided to the Land*
YHVH discarded for idols	*YHVH is "The Spring of Living Water"*
Israel broke the yoke of *YHVH*	*Israel had been planted a "living vine"*
Israel committed blasphemy	*YHVH will provide good shepherds*
Israel disdained its roots	*The Throne of God will be in Zion*
Sinners must repent	*YHVH will cure backsliding, sin*
Don't sow among the thorns	*YHVH will atone for sin*
Disaster follows you	*All nations can be won*
The earth will mourn	*Search for a holy one*
Your flocks, families devoured	*Even then: a remnant shall return!*
Israel has eyes but does not see	*I've given fertile land*
Disaster looms for Zion	*Seek the good way, walk in that path*
The wise are put to shame	*The Law gives wisdom*

Jerusalem will be laid waste	*YHVH will refine Israel*
Your fathers failed, so have you	*The desert promises will hold true*
The shepherds trample the fields	*YHVH's compassion brings you home*
A retribution waits	*Jeremiah will be saved, redeemed*
This nation: bereft of peace	*YHVH will restore His people*
Israel's true inheritance is lost	*Blessed are those who trust in God*

'Though some elements are missing, gentlemen, we've weighed in the balances, so to speak, the Problems and the Promises that we have found thus far in these discussions, fiery though they've been. What is the estimate? What do the scales of reckoning now prove?' the rabbi asked. 'The weight falls on the promises, Rabbi.' 'It is the promises that says it all for me, Sir.' 'I find the woe outweighs the wonder of the promises, Rabbi.' 'I cannot find agreement with that last assessment, Sir—look at those promises, Sir.' 'What better promises for a beleaguered land, Rabbi.' 'Can we hear the poem again?'

And so it was that for the present anyway, "The Prophet of Hope" had won the day. I was pleased to eat with Johanan that evening. I decided to share my problem with my best friend in the school. 'I had some idea that you had other interests claiming your attention. How you have kept your mind upon the unravelling of the holy scroll, I do not know. So, there is someone causing flutters on the brain! Who is the lucky lass, "My Man"? You cannot tell? A secret, not for general advertisement? You have my word. I will not blab! Not today? I'll bide my time—you'll weaken before the week is out!'

'Well, I know that you can hold your tongue when absolutely necessary. Joh, I've found my "soul-mate". There is no hope for us for Maryam is a half-sister of Herod Antipas!' Johanan all but choked upon his brew! He spluttered, coughed, and then: 'I see your problem, "My Man." Let's chew into the core it. From where I sit, I'd have to say that, so far as status goes, you haven't a hope in Heaven, Manaen, though you outclass the rest of us, a peasant scholar would not go down well among the coroneted heads parading in the palace of Herod Antipas!'

'I know it, Joh. It must end before it does begin.' 'Just wait a minute! I have not done with my advice. The palace is "no go" for peasants, lad. Agreed. Stay well away if that's to be the gauge for whether there's a happiness to be. I spoke of status. You could not mix with high society! But, my lad, with respect to character, you far outclass them all. I would advise a session with your mentor. He appears to hold a wise head on his shoulders; talk to him.'

As it happened, Nicodemus sought me out. He cut right through my quandary by stating, 'Manaen, I have been summoned to the Sanhedrin which—as you will know—is the supreme tribunal by which all questions regarding The Law are finally legislated; it is the Ruling Council of the Jews and headed by the High Priest. I will be leaving my role as tutor here to take up the prestigious position as a ruler of the Jews!'

Then, he staggered me. 'Manaen, I have observed your demeanour in class, your robust presentations, arguments well honed, innovative thinking—you swayed the class with your submission on a new title for Jeremiah. Well done, young man, well done!

'I have a request for you to think about—I've placed my application for an assistant scribe before the new Chief Rabbi, Annas. He has agreed. Annas is well informed as to your progress. He sees the logic of my choice. Manaen, would you consider becoming a student scribe? You would be assigned to me. All the practical aspects of your training will take precedence over your studies at the rabbinic school. What do you say? Would you like some time to consider the outcome before making your decision?'

'Nicodemus, Sir, what can I say? I'm rather overwhelmed. I have a basic idea of what that honoured role entails but could you, please, explain what would be expected of me?' 'You'll need to be well versed in the religious, civil and criminal laws of the land, being able to interpret the intricate nuances of each. As you become confident in your abilities, you may be expected to actually draft a legal document that I'll need to, for example, secure a sale of land, divide inheritance and the like.

'The written and the oral laws must be defined. I'll need you by my side at times to provide explanatory aspects of a case in hand. You will be expected to live by the standards set by The Law and the Prophets, interpreting the principles enshrined therein.'

'But, Nicodemus, surely, this is the role of the rabbis?' 'Not entirely so, young man! The rabbis teach The Law, a scribe must apply The Law! As you become adept, Manaen, you will be expected to travel to provincial cities as an inspector—observing the quality of the rabbis, and the standards by which the general populace lives, and moves and displays their ability to obey The Law.'

'Will I be required to join a political party? The Pharisees? The Sadducees?' 'It's better that you don't. Most scribes remain aloof as the bias of these parties can give an undue slant upon The Law and can sway a vote in favour of the most powerful voices in the court. Manaen, will you be my legal advisor in the Sanhedrin?'

Nicodemus must have seen the excitement welling up within his young prodigy. I smiled my acceptance together with the 'yea, Sir, yea!' He clasped my hand in confirmation of the agreement being ratified!

Another joy leapt in my heart! My pouch purse would be weightier now. Perhaps, enough to see a grin break out upon the face of Antipas, "The Quarter King" (Tetrarch, that is)! There was hope now in my stride as I took my leave of Nicodemus and made my way out through the Court of Men, through the Sheep Gate, northward past the Roman Fortress of Antonia. The Garrison was busy about its work but I steered clear of the cohort on duty there. Would I ever find a mind at ease when faced by the stern, iron fist of Rome? I hurried to my beloved with such happy news to tell!

Maryam received my confirmation ecstatically. My changed circumstance was received as a gift of grace! It could be done! We would become betrothed if only "big brother" would agree!

9. THE JERUSALEM PALACE

'Let's go to Antipas at once!' 'Dear heart, are you sure? I'll need to focus much attention on my new course. The life of a lawyer will make demands on me, on us!' 'Manaen, love of my life, I wish for no other way. Your life will be my life, your pain my pain, your aims my aims, your desires my desires and your joys my joys. Please come with me to the palace now.'

We walked together through the Northern Quarter, down to the arch which leads to the Upper City. The palace gates were opened quickly for the guards had seen Maryam's approach. The peasant had re-entered palace grounds—that belonging to Maryam's elder, half-brother Antipas, who deigned to welcome us.

Herod stared at me. 'So, *ben* of the Bethlehem shepherd, Baruch, let me look at you. You have grown up, I see, and none the worse for wear. A handsome man, as well! How did you manage that?' Yes, there was scorn in the voice of Antipas but something else was there as well. I think that Herod actually saw some hope in me. Perhaps there'd be some gain for him in the alliance of a scribe and princess! I read his petulance, his pride and his pandering!

It was time to speak. 'Herod, I have come today to ask for the
hand of the Princess Maryam in marriage, Sire. (How should I have
addressed a tetrarch? I had known him just as Antipas when we were
young lads at the Herodion). Antipas put on a thoughtful façade. He
ruminated on the quest. Maryam took a step forward, pleaded with her
brother there. Perhaps that's what Herod was waiting for. He smiled
his "Herod" smile. 'Although you do not present your backers—the
usual protocol for the betrothal, your request is granted, sister dear.
You are welcome here Manaen *ben* Baruch. The betrothal has been
accepted. 'You recognise of course that this agreement is binding on
you both! The Law declares—both legally and religiously—that you
are now man and wife though co-habitation will not be permitted
until, at this time next year, we celebrate your marriage here! You
may call Maryam your wife but—forget it at your peril—you cannot
break this bond unless through formal divorce proceedings. Manaen,
you may kiss your bride. I consider that you will give due regard to
her wellbeing. I charge you sincerely so to do!' I do believe that, for
once, Herod really meant what he had said. I think he truly cares for
his half-sister princess!

The man actually shook me by the hand—the only time I can recall
it ever happening. I was not in any way surprised that there was a certain
limpness in the clasp. But he seemed happy enough. I was prepared for
the discussion that arose as to the financial situation of the to-be groom.
Herod mentioned then his optimism that a scribe within the family-
fold would be advantageous and, of course, a fitting husband for his
favourite princess that was most appropriate! 'Have no fear, Manaen,
you will be no longer left "out in the cold"!' I thanked him then, gladly.
Our betrothal had begun!

My early exit from the rabbinic school came as a surprise to my
contemporaries (Johanan complained that he would be without "a limb
on which to lean"). The day was memorable in a number of ways. Just
to think of it still warms my heart towards our aged rabbi, Joseph *ben*
Jamin. All those centuries ago, *YHVH* had instructed Jeremiah to go

down to the local potter's *bayith* (house) to observe the man, his hands, his creation on the wheel and then discern what message could he bring to Israel, to Judah, to the world.

No, we did not go down to the potter's *bayith*: the potter came to us! There he was, his wheel made ready for our entrance to the room, a lump of clay was 'idling' on the wheel. We were called to attention and we were, in turn, brought up close to view the potter at his work. '*Ben* Baruch, now, take up the potter's task!' I paused. In shock, I think! And then I came to the wheel, sat upon the potter's stool, reached out my hands to mould the clay into, what I hoped would be something quite remarkable. I must admit the clay fell all about. My hands chased it, grabbed at it; I enclosed it in my trembling grip. The thing took shape. When I was done, there was a vessel formed but marred. There was a lack of symmetry, the base did not sit as well as I'd directed it. I cleansed my messy hands with due regret.

'What did you learn, *ben* Baruch?' 'Rabbi, I learned that the potter's hands are hurt by grit within the clay. No matter what its surface will convey, there's grit in the clay and it hurt my hand!' 'Well then, Manaen, what did you really learn?' 'It saddens me to think of how I may hurt the 'hands' of *YHVH* when there's grit within this mortal clay—*ME!*' 'When your vessel has been dried, you may come and claim your work for it will be a lasting memory in all your future days; make sure to keep the grit out of your life!'

The rabbi then addressed the class, 'Manaen *ben* Baruch will leave this school today. He is to become a scribe in training. He is to be the assistant of Nicodemus—the new appointee to the Sanhedrin as a ruler of the Jews. Stunned silence, of course. But then a happy chatter and some slaps upon my back relieved the shock of the news.

'Come, gentlemen. Let us turn our minds to a serious assessment of the prophecy of Jeremiah—is he, indeed, "The Prophet of Hope"? *Ben* Baruch has put forth the supposition that, over-riding everything the scroll puts out as devastating, ruinous, calamitous, Jeremiah is the prophet who declares—above all else—reason for our nation's hopefulness. By way of a final address, *ben* Baruch, support your thesis!

'May I begin at the potter's wheel, Rabbi?' The nod was all I needed to hold forth on what Jeremiah's grotto reflections had allowed me to realise. '*YHVH* spoke to Jeremiah at the potter's wheel, Sir. He said, *'See how, reshaped, the clay becomes a vessel of great grace and fit to serve the King!'* The LORD, *YHVH* emphasised that we are as the clay within His hands. Why is it, Sir, that we prefer the sodden mud? We should allow ourselves to be His vessels, fit for holy things. Why do we allow so much grit to hurt the Potter's hands?'

'A worthy prod, Manaen. What else have you to offer from your grotto meditations?' '*YHVH* declares that the day will come when He will raise a "Branch" from the vine of David; that He will be our King and He will reign in righteousness. And so much so that all Israel will sing for joy because *The LORD has now redeemed us from all alien governments.* What's more, Rabbi, *YHVH* promised to care for our people throughout the years of exile. He said, *I'll watch them, guard them, bring them home again. I'll build, not tear them down; I'll plant and not uproot. I'll give to My people then a heart that will recognise I AM the LORD. They will return to Me with all their heart, revived!*

'Rabbi, these promises are repeated through the scroll and then, *YHVH* declares, *You ask of Me why this gift of grace? I've loved you with an everlasting love, I've drawn you to Myself. You'll know My loving-kindness and you will be rebuilt. You'll shout your "Hallelujahs" yet for your joy will overflow!... There is a future after all the woes!*

'Rabbi, *YHVH* promised a new agreement between Himself and our people. He said: *This is the Covenant that I will make: I'll put My Law within your mind, I'll write it on your heart! I will forgive your wayward ways... My people will be healed and they will know My shalom peace. They will be cleansed. Then I will know their joy for their song shall be: 'Give thanks to YHVH El Shaddai for He is good and His love endures eternally.'*

A pandemonium broke out! How could it be like this when *YHVH*'s promises gave such occasion for great hope? 'Rabbi! I really must protest! This "about-to-be-lawyer, scribe", or what-ever, has not given appropriate balance to the promises by the just denunciations that flowed from the "lips" of *YHVH El Shaddai*!' Oh, yes! I might have known: the "Terror from Tarsus" is at his worst today! I swung at him with a vitriol I had not thought to use in any previous altercations which have broken out interminably in this room (it is the way with us). I gave no thought to wisdom's way. 'Why can't this upstart from the Diaspora give thought to the fact that the diatribes which abound in Jeremiah's scroll have been fulfilled. The split between the north and south: Judah and Israel! The Assyrian catastrophe! The seventy years of exile—the nation went to Babylon! The nation came back home!!! Then there was Greece! The tragedies of the Hasmoneans! The Roman conquest! Why can't Saul realise that it is the promises of God that reach down, through all the centuries, right down to us??? The Messiah is coming and, I feel it in my bones, very soon!!! He's nearer now than when Jeremiah gave us ground for *H.O.P.E.!!!*'

Applause broke out! Saul was "becalmed"! 'Rabbi, may I break with protocol to bring my last word to my fellow students and to you, whom I have grown to admire—your wisdom has guided me through this course. In the form of a lyric poem, may I bring a psalm to you all in a transformed style? You see, the rhythm is mixed up again with a metrical rhyme. But this is how the LORD impulses me to write, Rabbi.' Again, the applause—on this, the final day, a one-off acceptance of my "breakout" from the Hebrew forms of poetry. So, I began:

THE SONG OF JEREMIAH
(Choir: 7.7.7.7. e.g. Buckland)

LORD, You've known us from before
Birth had brought us into Light;
Plan of God before we breathed,
Set apart to tell Your might.

See a branch of almond tree
Burst to life in beauty rare;
Spring comes soon to those who trust:
Parable of Your great care.

There's a Balm in Gilead
Making wounded lives now whole;
Medicine to cure life's pain
Heals all grief that harms the soul.

Set up guideposts, mark the path
That will lead to faith's new start;
God will meet the seeking soul!
Stamp Your peace, LORD, on our heart.

Mould us as a potter forms
Clay within his skilful hand;
Shape us to Your pattern, LORD,
Make us vessels whole, as planned.

Blessing in abundance flows;
Great your Name, Your power is prime;
King of all the Earth, You rule:
LORD of all, You reign supreme.

We left the room in placated spirits and my closest friends sat with me at lunch before I went to Maryam with my news of the day.

10. TEMPLE COURTS AND COURTING RIGHTS

I have moved—from the minimal to the maximum—at the behest of Antipas. I think he wants to keep a "brotherly" eye on me! My humble quarters near the Rabbinic School have been exchanged for that of a rather lavishly styled abode situated in the Upper City. There were extra rooms. I could entertain visitors. I realised that this, the gift of the Tetrarch of Galilee—yes, Antipas—would be, within the year, my marriage *bayith*. I now lived in luxury! Maryam and I would settle into this new home! There was now no need to have concerns about my inability to care for her sufficiently—to the standards she had known.

Two things give a bother to me: I feel a segregation from my friends and, secondly, I am now living between *TWO* palaces: on the one hand, the memory of the long-departed Herod the Great (what a ghastly thought), and that of Herod Antipas. Fears and forebodings are tending to settle on my frame of mind whenever I view my immediate vicinity!

Donned in a new set of robes—I'm now an acknowledged 'citizen of high society'! My newly painted door was latched and I turned toward the Temple Courts. I faced the sun. The Temple was etched as a silhouette against the glory of the early morning light. Not Solomon, nor Herod, could erect a glorious structure to outshine the beauty of this dawn! This mount, these palms, this glorious light, are of God, the Creator of all things beautiful. Under the tutelage of Nicodemus, I would aim to keep things in true perspective. The power of Priests and Levites, of Pharisees and Sadducees, and yes, of Scribes as well, will be subservient—I hoped—to that of *YHVH El Shaddai*!

Coming now into the Temple courts I met with Nicodemus and he led me to the alcove that was his work station. There was a new desk there, in place for me. I felt elated! There was a parchment opened on the desk. We would come back to the work assigned. First of all, Nicodemus explained, a tour will be taken of the Hall of Hewn Stones where the Sanhedrin—the supreme legislative assembly of the Jewish nation—would sit to deliberate on the submissions of laws requiring ratification.

Upon entering the hallowed hall, I became aware of the orderly seating arrangements. Seventy-one chairs. Seventy-one (the odd number required, no doubt, to ensure a casting vote—that of the Chief Priest, without a doubt! We sat together there as Nicodemus explained the basics on how the Sanhedrin worked. After all, I was a student once again: a scribe in training to become an advocate in this hallowed Hall of Law.

We pondered the composition of the seventy men who sat before Annas, the High Priest. He claimed the paramount chair. The members of the Sanhedrin were, it was confirmed by my tutor, comprised of Pharisees, Sadducees, Priests, Levites and "ordinary" Jews as long as they belonged to the "right" families. The Sanhedrin was required to frame, to test and to activate laws linked to political, religious, and judicial matters brought to their attention by the populace—the public and the politicians themselves.

'But, Nicodemus, Sir,' 'Forget the "sir" when we're alone, Manaen!' 'Nicodemus, S…, er, Rome is in control of us. What are the parameters of legislation we may countenance?' 'As you well know, Manaen, the High Priest is recognised as the Civil Ruler of the nation. Politically, it is permitted for us to declare war!' 'War?' 'Manaen, this is a matter of theory *not* practice! There is another aspect linked with it, we may expand our territory—just think of Rome allowing that!' 'What then may be the things that we could bring about?'

'Manaen, you will discover that there are many prophets—even in the precincts of the Temple—who spit out false doctrines, a major problem in these parts! Then, there is quite a number of elders of the people who become recalcitrant. They rebel against the legal aspects of our laws. They stake their claims for the attention and the sanction of their complaint in the Sanhedrin.

'Always, we must keep in mind the values of The Law as handed down to Moses. It remains the sacred Law—it is sacrosanct! We work always within The Law. Our work is to certify subsidiary laws which are explanatory of the verities that must be obeyed always, in all ways! Let me illustrate, Manaen.

The laws we formulate must emulate The Law of *YHVH El Shaddai*. To put it another way, the laws that are presented to the Sanhedrin are, in reality, the rules and regulations that will *apply* The Law in practical terms, to given situations. There is such a claim that I must address this morning. Come, we will return to our desks in the Temple's Hall of Hewn Stones to start the work confronting us.'

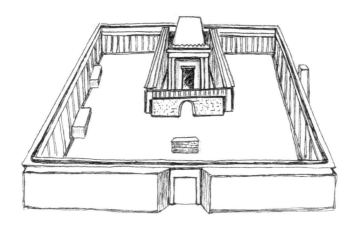

I placed my now 'venerable' writing kit upon my desk. I opened it to show to Nicodemus that I was ready for the task in hand. Was I? What was the problem now confronting us which would require the 'stitching together' of a law (a rule? a regulation?) that would require the legislative acumen of the Sanhedrin? I am becoming more aware that it is not so much The Law that is the vital issue: it is the matter of wrong-doing that requires The Law to be formulated in the first place!

'Manaen, there has been much speculation of late as to the length to which a man could go to rescue his donkey that has strayed, a goat caught in the gorse bush, a toddler son that skipped away from home. It is the *sabbath*—one can only move a certain distance, within the laws that govern this holy day. Our task is to determine if there are circumstances under which a man can overstep the mark set down in Law.' 'What is that distance, Nicodemus?' 'Two thousand cubits, no more—the measurement must be exact! The time-honoured basic cubit distance was determined in the olden days by aligning it with the space kept, most assiduously, from the Ark of the Covenant to those who marched behind the Holy Artefact when on Israel's pilgrimage toward the Promised Land.'

'It seems, to my understanding, that this cannot be altered— to overstep the mark would mean the breaking of the Holy Law, Nicodemus.' 'Well, not necessarily so, young man! There has been quite a 'to do' in the Sanhedrin as to the possibility of setting up a temporary *bayith* at the extremity of what is allowed and call it "home"!' 'You mean, walk the two thousand cubits from home, as allowed by The Law, and then build another *bayith*?' 'Not at all. Just place a home object, a meal for example, upon the ground at the extremity of what is allowed by Law and march right up to it. Then, one could start again to count off two thousand cubits in order to retrieve the donkey, catch the goat!

'The various alternatives could make a mockery of the Law! Here is a list. I ask that you will give due diligence to the alternatives and frame some thoughts for a submission which is to be presented to the Sanhedrin, say—before the *sabbath*. And Manaen, don't make a "*sabbath* journey" of your work!' I smiled at his intended joke!

I worked at it, wrestled with the pros and cons, riled on the alternatives and, before my eyelids claimed their rest, I felt that I had given an adequate response. Nicodemus thought so too. He considered the ramifications of:

> The Law is sacrosanct. Israel must adhere to its every requirement.
> YHVH is compassionate. He understands a poor man's plight.
> He will expect an honest farmer to give every care to his flock.
> Exceptions must be allowed when toddlers have gone astray.
> The Law will stand; exceptions will prove its worth.

I was invited to the Sanhedrin on the day that Nicodemus was to present the case for clemency in the face of dire distress. My presence in the great assembly was acknowledged before the actual presentation commenced. I listened so attentively; after all, the content turned out to be, largely, framed by my own input! To our regret, the law was not passed. There were to be no amendments to the "sacred text"! To my chagrin, this meant that the Sanhedrin would turn a blind eye to the infringements. But the lowly farmer, in his extremity of need, would still be "the sinner" while dearly loved by *YHVH El Shaddai*! Let forgiveness rest with Him, then. It would be enough!

Life in the Upper City continued with its blessings and its bane! I could stroll with Maryam, even visit her at the palace with no embargo on my entry through the gates! Antipas was frequently in town. He loved to party, celebrate his return with his dubious friends. Yes, he was the "visitor". His jurisdiction was the Galilee and peripheries—the "quarter king" in fact, actually the Tetrarch of the Galilean region. I loathed the idea of sitting at the drunken tables of the "Royal Receptionist" where the wine flowed over-freely through the night.

My one personal pleasure at these events was, of course, that Maryam sat at my side. Our focus was confined to conversations about our todays and our tomorrows. We also held the others' hand for our unspoken conversations of the night as well! We, the betrothed, made the most of these occasions and went to our separate abodes untainted by the debauchery surrounding us.

At first, we'd thought, this year would never end but it moved on apace. The need to plan ahead was becoming paramount. There would need to be some adequate arrangements so that my aged parents, Yehudith and Baruch could attend. The journey to Jerusalem would challenge them but it could be done, including their accommodation.

Would we abide by the time-honoured traditions regarding the consummation of our betrothal or, would we make our own way through the marriage night? Yes, there were aspects we would not change. There would indeed be the procession by the groom; the canopy celebration would be performed; the wearing of the *kattel* (the garment of white linen). Because the bride's father, Herod the Great was dead, we thought it still appropriate that I should present the *brideworth gift*. It would need to be handed to Antipas. What, possibly, could I give to the Tetrarch of Galilee? This would exercise my brain. Perhaps Nicodemus could give some helpful advice.

The *ketubah* (marriage contract), would be signed by my selected witnesses… Lets, see. Of course: Johanan and Nicodemus. The *chuppah* (marriage canopy) would be in place. I would present my ring to her. There'd be the broken cup! We would request that Rabbi Joseph *ben* Jamin pray a blessing on our marriage. There would be a feast and dancing through the night.

We both agreed to forego—with no doubts from either the bride or groom—the usual practice of placing a white linen sheet upon the marriage bed for later inspection. The invariably assembled throng outside the room could then prove the validity of the bride's purity until the actual consummation of the marriage! Blood upon the sheet would suffice to satisfy the inquisitors.

The bride and groom planned to slip away into what would be our shared *bayith* and bed. No one would notice our departure if we waited until after the *horah* dance during which we would be held aloft for all to prance about with glee. We smiled our mutual agreement into the other's eyes and sealed it with our kiss.

84

'Manaen, you've done some personal study on the life and times of the prophet Ezekiel. I'd like to discuss with you some deep concerns that, as a Pharisee, I must confirm. My brain is not in line with the soul's response to his prophecies. Come, chat a while.'

'I must confess, there is no real depth to my scant understanding of his epic work, Nicodemus, but I'd be glad to share with you my reactions to the many conundrums found in his writings. I have some questions too.' 'That's what I thought, young man. When two minds come to a mystery with a serious intensity, there's bound to be some helpful outcomes. Let me lay it on the line: We Pharisees believe that we will live on after death occurs. The Sadducees are adamant: they don't! Quite frankly, I believe this is a battle between the theists and the atheists! Where would you go into Ezekiel's proclamations that can give some weight to the propositions I must make?' 'What is the major quandary?' 'It's this: the matter of a life beyond the grave.'

'Nicodemus, it is late in the work that we can have our best results.' 'Ah, I think that you agree with me. Have you cast your mind to the section on "The Valley of Dry Bones"?' I smiled a happy smile at him. 'I have indeed!' I went right to the heart of Ezekiel's vision (well, not quite! These were dry bones). But on with it, *ben* Baruch: *YHVH* speaks with Ezekiel, exiled as he was, away in Babylon:

'*O son of man* (what a lovely title, Nicodemus. We'll never hear the like of that again), *O son of man,* He said*, It is time to bring a word of comfort to Israel… Tell Israel that they will come home… New fruit will form on every spreading tree. The people will increase. They'll be renewed… Then all will know I AM, the YHVH Elohim… I'll sprinkle you with water that is pure, you will be cleansed… I will remove your heart of stone, replacing it with tenderness… My Spirit will reside in you…*

'Yes, yes. I know it well. But I have serious questions that remain. How does the *ruach* Spirit of Eternal God bring about renewal in people's lives? There's much I'd like to know about that mystery. Perhaps, one day… But, Manaen, the bones, the dry bones?'

'Nicodemus, I have already made so bold as to write a poem based on Ezekiel's unique vision—a mystery, indeed, but there is an utter truth concealed within that prophecy. Perhaps, together, we can search it out through the telling of the poem to simplify the core of it.'

DRY BONES?

Dry bones, dry bones, within
an arid place, a valley of despair
where life ne'er comes!
These desert sands exposed its dearth.

The Spirit of the YHVH, LORD
has brought me to this barrenness.
He spoke to me: 'O son of man,
could these bones, dry bones live?'
How could I answer Him?
I ceded to His wisdom, said:
'O Sovereign LORD, alone you know!'
'So, son of man, now prophesy
unto these bones: 'Dry bones,
now hear the voice of YHVH, LORD:
Hark! Listen, bleached bones now:
the LORD will send His Spirit-Breath
to you, to enter you and you will live.
New tendons will attach to flesh,
the bones will be aligned with bone.'

Then, as I looked, I saw indeed
a miracle take form before
my startled gaze. The form
was there but, where was life?

'O son of man, now prophesy:
This is what the LORD declares:
Come from the winds, four winds

of Earth: O Spirit-Breath.
Now breathe upon these slain
that they may live!'

Those lifeless forms
began to move, they stood
upon their feet. They danced
with joy: this army lived again!
'O son of man', He said: 'Observe.
Here stands the House of Israel,
renewed, made whole once more.
Now, say to Israel: Your graves
will open, I will bring you up
from them. You'll live again!
My Spirit will reside in you;
you'll settle in your land,
the land of Israel. Then you
will know I AM, the LORD!
(Ezekiel 37:1-14)

We sat a while in silence, mulling on this mystery that should be plain to us. Nicodemus spoke at last. 'I've studied this prophecy for years. There are concerns in the text though you have clarified so much of it. Yes! there must in fact be the possibility of life following on after death! *YHVH* would not speak a promise that is not based upon a fact. And *YHVH* really likes that phrase, "son of man". I wonder why? But there are larger matters to digest. I am amazed by what the *ruach* Spirit of the LORD will be able to do with a nation of "dry bones". How will He "breathe His Life" in us? Is there any hope for Israel? For the "two" to be entwined again to become one branch? Ezekiel knew it could. But how? When will we see the end of the "New Babylon"—Rome?!' 'Ah, Nicodemus, you ask *when*, not *if*!' This cheers my heart!'

'Manaen, I fear that Ezekiel has thrown another mystery at us—a greater mystery which I am afraid to even think about!' 'What could be a larger mystery than "The Valley of Dry Bones", Nicodemus? Let us think about it. Wondering together may bring some answers for your grief about this thing that plagues you so.' 'Manaen, I have not long returned from Samaria. The journey there was pleasant enough. A rough ride, it is true. The donkey was not pleased with the weight he had to carry all the way. The project finally complete, I started out upon the homeward journey.

'As I approached Jerusalem, I came across great poles implanted in the ground. Atop the poles were cross bars nailed to the wood. And, on each frame, there was a man, writhing in agony or still, in death. I've never seen the like of it. I'd heard, you see, that these are scaffolds on which a criminal would be staked until his death. Naked, bloody, men in agony until death claimed them, bringing their final release. There was a stench that seemed to follow me along the mountain trail.

'This is Rome's new way of ridding their great empire of any who dare to challenge them. Never has there been a more treacherous means of ultimate punishment for crime than this vile instrument of death. I fear I've seen a veiled description of this scaffold in a vision seen, yes: hundreds of years before Rome marched over our borders, to Jerusalem. Can you recall, for me, a memory of such a vision, Manaen? Think. When did a vision take Ezekiel from Babylon, back into Jerusalem?'

'I can think of one such instance but there is no connection there with what you have seen so near Jerusalem.' 'What is the vision that is stuck in your memory? Come, think of it. Tell me what Ezekiel saw.' 'Nicodemus, that vision had to do with the desecration of King Solomon's Temple.' 'Yes! Yes! go on!'

'Well, Ezekiel is sitting in his home with the captive Jewish elders gathered there. Ezekiel looks up to see a being shining just like molten metal. He lifts the prophet and transports him to Jerusalem by means of the vision. Ezekiel is carried to Jerusalem just in the deepest regions of his soul, I presume. This was a powerful vision, Nicodemus.' 'Go on! What happens then?' 'Ezekiel is standing there in the precincts of the Temple. He is shown some ghastly scenes where gaudy idols were worshipped. His guide instructs him to go through an opened door to observe the blasphemies being perpetrated in the Holy Place. Ezekiel is horrified by his vision now! He sees some guards together with a scribe who is dressed in purest linen. He notices that the scribe is carrying a writing kit.'

'This vision is beginning to enlighten me. Go on, Manaen: the reason for the writing kit?' 'The glory of the LORD arises and moves right to the threshold of the Temple. *YHVH* gives instruction to the scribe: *Go through Jerusalem and prepare to place the mark of 'tav' upon the foreheads of all those who grieve, lamenting the idolatry so rampant in Jerusalem. The guards accompanying the scribe are then instructed to slay all those that do not wear that mark upon their foreheads. Begin within the Sanctuary.*

'But, Nicodemus, I do not see the significance this vision has with regard to that ghastly sight you came across when returning to Jerusalem so recently.'

'I do! I do. I see it all. I weep again for our Jerusalem!' 'How so, Nicodemus, how so?' 'Manaen, place the mark of the *tav* upon your parchment there.' I took up my writing tool and wrote with ease, the final letter of our Hebrew alphabet: ת. 'There is a significance?' 'Oh yes!' 'It never has been clearer than right now. Set down, for me, the more ancient form of *tav*, Manaen. I was aghast. The ancient sign of *tav* was exactly in the shape of a †! It was the very shape of the Roman scaffolds which Nicodemus had seen on his homeward journey from Samaria! Those cross shaped scaffolds were never used until the Romans introduced their hideous form of execution. How could it have been that Ezekiel "saw" a cross upon the foreheads of those who had remained true to *YHVH* and that it was the very means by which they would be saved, redeemed!? This was too much for us. *O Eloi, Eloi!*

'Manaen *ben* Baruch, your prayer is eloquent! 'You speak, of course, of King David's grievous prayer. King David is, beyond his knowledge, providing a detailed description of the Roman scaffold on which, as I have witnessed, all criminals who will be from this time on condemned to death, hung out on those cross-beams. He "witnessed" this ghastly sight hundreds of years before its time!

'Manaen, I fear now for what King David's psalm may be really describing. It may be warning us of one nailed to a cross as the ultimate punishment for crimes he would not commit; one who would be wholly innocent! Do you have time, Manaen, to share with me the outcome of your studies on that psalm—the one commencing *Eloi, Eloi…?*'

'But Nicodemus, why are you in such obvious mental anguish over what our analysis of the psalm might reveal to us?' 'It is the possible identity of the one who is voicing those agonising word-pictures. It is as though an innocent man will go to his death to prove his identity!' 'If it wasn't David, who would be a "king" giving up his life?' 'A son of David. A "Son of David"?'

'Oh no! Manaen! This could mean that it is the *Messiah* who will be slaughtered—the most innocent for the most guilty!' 'Be calm in your soul, Nicodemus, Sir! It can't be the *Mashiach*—he will be the "Beloved of the LORD". *YHVH* would not send, let's say, "The Prince of Heaven" to his death for the likes of us! We can rest assured of that.' 'I agree! Yet–somehow–I do think that *YHVH* is involved and that sin cannot be erased without a sacrifice.' 'We're well aware of that: look at the daily sacrifice… the *Yom Kippur*—the Day of Atonement.' 'Yes, there'll be a sacrifice like no other we have seen.

'Please, my young friend, please: let us begin. What does the psalmist say?' I had to think for a while. Then, conversing all the while, we placed these comments on the parchment as they came to mind:

Eloi, Eloi… My God, why?
The innocent feels forsaken
His prayer remains unanswered
He is scorned and ridiculed
Recognition: YHVH gave him life

The plea now for His help
His life is seeping away—like water
His bones are out of joint
His heart is melting —like wax
His strength has dried—like a broken vase
He 'lays in the dust of death'
His hands and feet are pierced
People stand and stare at him
'They' divide, cast lots for his clothes
His prayer: 'come quickly, deliver me
He will 'declare' YHVH's name, give praise!
YHVH has not despised him, not hidden Face
Through Him, all the ends of the Earth: know!
They will remember, turn to YHVH, LORD!
The LORD rules over all the nations.
Future generations will know it is "The Lord"
All will proclaim his righteous sacrifice (Psalm 2:

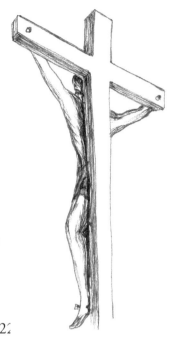

The days, weeks and months dragged on. But there were highlights that could please the hardest heart. Let it be said, to my great satisfaction, that—between the two of us, the 'master' and his lad—there were quite a number of by-laws passed in the Supreme Council of Justice. Nicodemus is becoming adept at the swaying of entrenched opinions. Where his submissions kept The Law as sacrosanct, there have been some new ideas to which the Sanhedrin could turn a friendly eye and did, with decisions made that were wholly circumspect.

Nicodemus would berate, at times, the rigidity of laws that failed their best intent. He would lament that even the Holy Law scratched on those slabs of stone encased below the Mercy Seat—the *caphah* lid of the Ark of the Covenant—could never change the evil ways of humankind who would defy, defile the sacred text of Law. 'The Law points to the sin, the crime. It cannot rectify the circumstance, make right the consequence,' he'd say. 'There is something deeper, more profound than Law, that's needed for the recompense! What is it that could break the Law open, release its best intent? The loving-kindness of the LORD! A word we want, a word we need to illustrate the loving-kindness of the LORD! Think on it, Manaen. Bring me something that will ease my mind! Don't harm the slabs that carry The Law but tell me what will change the status quo. The Law is given to guide us but it cannot change us! Find me something that will!' We mulled on the matter.

What could it possibly be? *Gracious*! The time. The time! I hear the noon-day ram's horn. It is time for me to flee! Tomorrow is "the day of days" for Maryam and me... *Gracious*? GRACE! That is the word. But where to find the word. It's there! It's there! Colouring all the history of The Law! It's there, in Genesis! And, think of Exodus! What grace there is in Exodus! Judges... Ruth! Oh yes! The alien bride for Boaz found in the fields near Bethlehem! The Psalms... so much Grace, it overflows! The Prophets? Enough and to spare! I can't wait till I tell Nicodemus!

The day was long. So very long. Much longer, it seemed, than the hours crammed in that day. This is our wedding day. Our wedding night! *Em* and a*bba* (my parents, Yehudith and Baruch) had managed the journey and were clearly excited that their son would be married before the day was done. And, one day ("soon" they did pronounce), there would be a son—a child to gladden their elderly hearts.

Maryam would be attended by her ten bridesmaids. And, when all was in readiness, the maids would go—according to custom—out into the night carrying their lanterns to light the way for the groom so impatient now to be on his way to meet the bride! Oh! here they come. My robe, my robe! Is it set on straight? Be calm... *Shalom* to me, I thought.

There was the canopy. Here is my bride. Regal. Beautiful. So soon, wholly mine! The ring? Where is the ring? Ha! There it is. On my finger... Be calm Manaen. Still your jitters, man! Herod, the "quarter king" was actually standing to attention there! Beside me now, my two witnesses—Johanan and Nicodemus—both looking extremely pleased with themselves. *Em* and *abba* too (I think there were a tear or two)! And me? How were my thoughts displayed? Tearful joy, I think!

I place the ring on her slender hand. The cup was thrown to the floor. It smashed—as well it should! Rabbi Joseph prayed a blessing on the bride and groom. We sealed our marriage there with a holy kiss!

The celebrations had begun. Dancing, eating, drinking, chattering, chanting. The night wore on. Soon, demands would be placed upon the married pair. Hurry on, the rising of the bride and groom upon the shoulders of the rowdy throng! We'd take our chance then, as planned, to slip away without an eye to capture us. It worked! There would be no inspection of our marriage bed!

We had no need for bridesmaid lanterns now. I knew the way. The gift of Antipas ensured that this bride and groom, this man and wife, would always be tied-down to palaces! Our *bayith*, located as it was, between the two palaces in the Upper City, would make quite sure of that. The one relent, a kindly act, I think, was to offer us some little time down at the winter palace at Jericho. We received that marriage gift with thanks.

Maryam had been quiet, almost silent, through the celebrations in the Palace of Antipas but the way she clung so firmly to my hand upon the path leading to our home, left me in no doubt that the quietness masked no fear. Maryam was coming to terms with her new status. The princess had married the peasant and, somehow, I knew she was glad.

Upon entering our *bayith*, I found that the candles lit up with ease. (Why, Manaen, your hand is steady; how come when you are on the edge of new miracles?) Here was the moment for which we had yearned those lonely years, those hopeful, hopeless, hopeful years. We stand together, savouring the love that flows from eyes to eyes. We help each other with the robes… We sense where our desires lay… I lift my bride and take her to our bed.

I had not thought to find a bliss such as this: arms with arms, lips with lips, body with body: one! And, in the deep, warm darkness of the night, I gifted her our coming child.

The morning found me, surprisingly, alert. Maryam slept on. I would not waken her yet. There had been so little sleep, so little rest in the night. I rose. Went to my writing kit. Some prose, perhaps? But no, the language flowed into the poetry a lover knows when seeking to place in words, the devotion, the dedication, he will give to the marriage. I knew that it required a prayer:

"FOR MARYAM"

Day of rejoicing,
Moment of blessing,
Hour when are sanctified
The vows of love's union
Sealed at this altar,

Heart and hand ever entwined.
What shall I pray for you,
How shall I speak for you?
O LORD, this marriage bless;
Grant each Your guidance,
Enduring patience:
LORD of Love,
Grant faithfulness.

Day of enrichment,
Moment so hallowed,
Hour when the future is sealed;
How swift will time fly
Into tomorrow:
For that day is grace revealed.
This shall I pray for you,
Here will I plead for you:
May grace outweigh your cares,
Hope bring you courage,
Faith be your anchorage;
Love Divine,
This gift God shares.
Day for remembrance,
Moment enduring,
Hour when we celebrate
A dawning future
Rich in love's sharing,
Radiating Heaven's own Light.
This would I speak for you,
As now I pray for you:
O LORD, Your aid bestow,
By Your own virtue
This union nurture;
Abiding Love,
These lives o'erflow.

Day of commitment,
Moment compelling,
Hour of love's pledging complete,
As vows well-cherished,
Spoken before Him
Echo now in lives replete.
Here will I speak for you,
Now make my prayer for you:
May peace attend your ways,
Joy meet your 'morrow,
Soothe every sorrow;
Eternal Love,
Grant love always.

I moved to our bed, wakened Maryam with my lips, my hands. Her deep, dark eyes looked up, a little dazed, I think. There was a question there. It swiftly went. Maryam smiled at me and raised her arms... After an enraptured morning, I read the prayer poem to her. Maryam had no words for me but showed her gladness in my arms. Such things as breakfast were put on hold. But, finally, the princess and her peasant ate most happily.

The gift of Antipas, granting Maryam and me an entry to the winter palace at Jericho, was taken up with glee. As soon as practical, husband and wife descended the mountains and found themselves luxuriating in what was still a magnificent edifice even though its 'architect' (Herod the Great) was now long gone.

We walked, and talked. We wallowed in the pool filled to grant us true delight. We ate, we slept. What ease was this! It could not go on. There was work awaiting me. First though, we took a journey to the great Salt Sea. Quite "dead", of course, but starkly magnificent. We managed a brief glance or two at the sparse establishment built to enclose the Essenes by the shoreline. We swam. Not really! How can I put it best? We floated? I suppose, but... really, we just sat upon the water! That's right, more *on* than *in* the water! We found the salt, and all the accumulated minerals from eras past, to be so dense (the water tending toward a syrup, almost), we "sat" upon the waters there until the sun won the day. We sought some shade. Then, on to the palace and its cool welcome.

The last of our "holy days" at the winter palace at Jericho found us in the luxuriant garden, date palms waving in the desert breeze and granting us the shedding of their fruit. What memories emerged of our earliest times together as children in the garden of the Herodion.

We walked on to the ancient Tel of Jericho. We searched for artefacts. There were so few. The ruination of this once walled city of great repute was caused by marching, marching feet. For seven days, the march around the city of Jericho. Then, on the seventh, seven times the march. The walls came tumbling down. And fire broke out. Yes, still there was the hint of ash, of coal, deep in the lower levels of the mound.

'Look at this, Maryam! The history of our people is written here. Joshua fought the battle of Jericho and—with the help of *YHVH*—won!'

'Manaen, I am not wholly of your ancestry. But, dear heart, your people have become my people and *YHVH* is truly now my God. We are ONE, dear heart. We are ONE! Let there be no division in our thinking, in our doing, in our feelings or our faith!'

How soon it was (too soon, it seemed), that I returned to the alcove of Nicodemus to resume the tasks accumulating on his desk and mine!

'How have you fared, Manaen? I must say, you look none the worse for wear and tear!' 'It's truly been a time of wedded wonder, Nicodemus! It is as though the moon has shared its honey just for us!' 'My friend, I trust that the "honey" from that "moon" will never cease its flow to you!' I saw a hint of humour play about his kindly face as we clasped hands in a firm grip. Then the work began, the pile of parchments was high.

11. THE REUNION

Our son was born in the spring. By then, the almond blossom had given of its best and now was into fruiting on the bough. It had been a difficult birth. *Emi* and *abbi* were present. *Emi*—the *yalad* of great experience—knew how to manage things far more than most. We had utmost faith in her expertise. Maryam knew full well that *emi* had tended Herod's birthing queens—the multiple queens—at the Herodion. Maryam and my Mother went together into the birthing room. Hours, agonising hours, passed.

Abbi and I talked incessantly of the days of long ago in Bethlehem, of lambing in the hills. Did I remember the stable birth? We wondered what had become of my young *kebaa-baa-baas* "Lamb". 'I think, *abbi*, that he will return one day—just like he did in the Temple as a twelve-year old. I think he lives in Galilee… Probably taken over his *abba's* carpentry business by now.' Joseph was no "spring lamb" when little *Yeshua* was born amongst the songs of angel choirs and stable grime!

The cries began again. More faint. I must go to her! But wait, is that a baby's cry I heard? My a*bbi* slapped me on the back. 'You are an *abba* now, my son!'

Emi came to me with my swaddled son. I was in awe of him, my child. 'Go to her, Manaen. Her time was long; the birthing, difficult. She'll need your arms, now, to comfort her.' In entering the room, I saw a weariness upon my beloved's face I'd never known before. Why is a birthing so very painful, so excruciatingly difficult?

'Maryam, my love, we have a son. What shall we name our child?' 'His name will be David… Let him remember, as he grows, the value of Jewish history. O Manaen, may our son follow in the footsteps of the best of kings! My dear, *abba* of our son: I'm tired, so tired… tir…'

The time has sped on. I swear I have noted a grey hair or two emerging from the beard I wear. Maryam is quite amused, but yet enamoured by those streaks of grey. Though I'd spread it not abroad, I have discovered, above her brow, some streaks of grey akin to mine. Let's grow old together Maryam!

Apart from teething troubles, a grazed knee or two, our son was gaining strength. It had needed extra care to nurture him. His baby days had been impacted by the difficult birth. Maryam is a wonderful Mother. She tests her skills of training young David in ways whereby his *abba* would be proud. The largest burden of nurturing and the disciplining of our son fell upon her as I was now called away for inspection tours more frequently. I did try to make up for this when I returned and was able to spend some time with him.

My challenge was to make certain that I would not spoil the child—leave the discipline to his Mother, save the playtime just for me! Somehow, we managed fairly well. Apart from a few boyhood blubbers, we made a go of it. The boy would sometimes preen himself with a play-time coronet upon his youthful crop of hair. He called himself "the half-prince" in fun, I'd hoped. I prayed for him—that he would follow in the steps of the Bethlehem shepherd and not those of the dissipated "quarter king". Young David would soon be old enough to join the Temple's Rabbinic School!

'My love, school me in the things that I should know about the Messiah. We did not know of *Mashiach* in the palace. We did not frequent the synagogue. I hear you speak of him. I need to know.' I took Maryam's request most seriously and set about sharing what the holy texts have revealed to our people. We spoke of it when David was at play with his friends.

One morning, Maryam shocked me with her response to something I had shared with her about the Messiah. I think I'd mentioned that I felt that his coming was near. 'Manaen, I fear for the Messiah and I fear for you!' 'Dear heart, what do you mean?' 'I fear that our people will turn their backs on him and laugh him to scorn!' 'Whatever makes you think such a thing?' 'The texts you read to me, Manaen; the texts you read. Remember what Isaiah said, *He was despised and rejected, a man of sorrows and acquainted with grief. And we hid our face from him… The LORD has laid on him all our iniquities.*

Eloi, Eloi, what could I say to that? Has Maryam become a prophet in our day? I calmed her then by sharing with her the conclusion of Isaiah's words: *Therefore, YHVH has highly exalted him and given him a name above all names… Every knee will bow to him.* 'Maryam, we need to know his *shalom* peace!' 'What is so special about *shalom?*'

'*Shalom* peace doesn't wait for absence of strife. It knows serenity in the midst of strife for *Shalom* is peace of heart.' 'Then *shalom* is enough for me!' Yes, we are at peace.

Nicodemus came to me with, 'Manaen, the high Priest's "feathers" have been ruffled! There have been many rumours and inuendoes coming up from the Jordan River area, down near the Salt Sea. It does appear that there is a man of the desert feeding minds with ideas alien to the way of things in Jerusalem and the Temple, in particular. He is baptising many there. People journey from all about to be "water-blessed". We need to ensure that the obvious proselytising is *kosher* (proper)! Things must adhere to what has been set down in The Law!

'Something must be done. We'll need an extensive report. Can you spare the time?' 'Nicodemus, this sounds intriguing, most curious. I'd like to be involved.' I packed my satchel right away, bid farewell to Maryam, ruffled up the already unruly hair of my son and heir and challenged him, on pain of stern chastisement (verbal, of course), upon my return if he had failed to please his kind and ever-loving mother!

The trek down through the mountains from Jerusalem does not get easier! It's all quite dangerous, really, prone to attack by robbers. As the ground levels out near Jericho, the journey is all but done. I found a lodging house to rest overnight for the mission would be challenging, to say the least of it. Now, where should I begin? Ask this? Say that? Had I thought to rest tonight?

By noon, the river was in sight. Now, that was surprising. Here I was, on the edge of the desert, and there were people everywhere. Their differing modes of dress revealed that they had come from near and far. And there were the rich, the poor. I thought that the baptiser could be close by! My mission had begun.

Engaging in conversation, I discovered some fascinating facts! Man of the desert he may well be, but this John—his name by the way—was, would you believe, actually a priest! His father, I gather, was a man by the name of Zechariah who belonged to the priestly division known as that of Abijah. He and his wife, Elizabeth, I'm told, lived in the hill country of Judea. Zechariah was a righteous, law-abiding man. 'How come the son is clothed, I'm told, in a camel's hide?' 'His parents were very elderly when he was born. He became an orphan when quite young and there was no one to care for him.' Another said, 'The desert has done no harm to him; he is a strong and sturdy man—locusts and wild honey have gone down well for him.' 'Look at him! There he is by the water's edge.'

Approaching through the crowd, I came to the verge of the river. Here, I saw another man, waist deep in the stream. He appeared to be meditating, perhaps at prayer.

A dove paused in flight just above the man's head and hovered there as if listening in to the prayer. The man seemed unaware of it. I had seen enough. I could return to Jerusalem and present my findings to Nicodemus. Wait till he hears about the priesthood!

I turned to leave, looking to the hills from whence I'd come. I had the answers or, so I'd thought. The voice I heard was that of the desert man. Hoarse, somewhat coarse, but what he said would change my life! 'BEHOLD: HERE IS "THE LAMB OF GOD"! HE WILL REMOVE ALL SIN!'

"The *Lamb*"? I turned again. I stared at him. Is it…? Could it be…? He smiled in his approach to me. Now even John the baptiser looked on. He had recognised me already. He smiled at me! I'd found my friend!

'*Yeshua!*' It's you! It's really you!' 'My friend. I knew you'd come!' 'What? How could…?' He smiled at me! '*Kebes!* "The Lamb of God!"' I am speechless! 'Manaen, we must share our news. It's not possible just yet. The road ahead for me is strewn with rocks. But I will come to you.' '*Yeshua*, I've so much to tell you. I am married now. Maryam, my wife, is a princess from the Herodion. I love her so! We have a son, *Yeshua*. He is David *ben* Manaen!' 'What wonderful news! I rejoice with you!

Manaen, call me *Jesus* now. You'll see the reason on a special day! Expect to see me soon!' Then, he returned to John the baptiser.

I went to a solitary place to contemplate what I had heard, what I had seen. I opened up my writing kit, intending to record my findings. I began to write. The thought of him, Jesus, intruded. Jesus! "The Lamb of God"? The Lamb… ?

THE LAMB

A gentle lamb,
Fragile, not free:
Made so vulnerable—
***Trusting** yet the lamb will be.*

As a yielding lamb
Before its shearers: bait,
Silent, still, remains
***Accepting** of its fate.*

Led to untimely death,
Unto its slaughter moves;
A lamb struck down,
***Giving** life for other lives.*

The blood flows now:
On ebb, the lamb–unsoiled–
Is fit for sacrifice,
***Cleansing** sins for all the world.*

The Mercy Seat
Is stained with blood:
The Ark of Covenant
***Receiving** sacrifice to God.*

Blood of a lamb
With High Priestly cants

Could bring about
Atoning *circumstance?*

Can lambs provide
A fitting sacrifice
For sin, or is this act
Symbolising *greater sacrifice?*

Behold the Lamb:
"The Lamb of God" will be
The Symbol now
Solidifying *true Reality!*

I closed my writing kit, many questions yet playing about in my mind but also some answers were forming there. I felt convinced that Jesus would solidify my restless questioning. *Eloi, Eloi,* speed the day when I can meet with *Yeshua*–Jesus again!

I've rarely seen Nicodemus in a more elated frame of mind. He took my report concerning the Jordan River baptisms very seriously but also absorbed my poem with a respect that pleased me very much. I felt that he concurred with my own sentiments. We really were a team! We set ourselves to the task of framing the final report that had been honed to a brevity which would be pleasing to the Sanhedrin.

To gather to myself Maryam's loving welcome home was even more pleasing. And David had, upon his maturing face, a happy grin confirming that he and she had bided well in the interim! It took some time to tell of the Jordan event adequately. Even David chimed in with questions and comments that revealed my son's growing interest in the affairs of state which demanded so much of my time and attention!

There were occasions when the aged Rabbi Joseph *ben* Jamin would call me to the Rabbinic School to air my views on this and that. As is usually the way of things in that revered room, there was the toing and froing of those for or against the propositions placed at their "disposal", so to speak. The first morning's rankling was spectacular! I had been asked to share my thoughts on the Jordan experience. I took the liberty of sharing the lines which I had written in such haste following the event. The *Trusting… Accepting… Giving… Cleansing… Receiving… Atoning… Symbolising… Solidifying…* became too much for those lads. Even the rabbi found it difficult to handle the debate.

One morning, I was called to the school to present a parchment on "The Messiah". Surely, there could not be a more contentious subject. What? When? Where? Why? How? How could I expect to address, with wisdom (belying my years) and astute acumen, such a convoluted topic? Where could I begin? Let's set them on their ears: I'll start in Genesis! Why, one may ask? Well, there, in the earliest accounts of life after Eden, I believe the first promise of "The Coming One" was given. Look it up, if you dare. Don't worry, I'll announce it here:

הוא ישופך ראש ואתה תשופנן עקב

He will bruise you to the head and you will bruise of him the heel.
Genesis 3:15

'What do you mean?' 'What on Earth does a head and a heel have to do with it?' Questions came, answers came—from me! 'Think of the context, young man! You'll find your answer there! Head? Heel? Where would you prefer to receive a wound? That's right. The "attacker" will receive the fatal blow! But, mark you well, though the Promised One, the "responder", will also be wounded in the battle, finally, He will live to show his wounds, to affirm his final victory.

We scanned the Major—and the Minor—Prophets, sometimes with joy, sometimes with due alarm. I felt as though I had become a part-time rabbi when I handed over the charcoal for a student to commence a list under the heading of, "The Messiah—The Anointed of God". As we shared the promises, a "telling picture" emerged.

THE MESSIAH—THE ANOINTED OF GOD

The descendant of Abraham:	Genesis 12:3, 17:19
All nations will be drawn to him	Genesis 28:14, Isaiah 11:10
He will be known as the Passover Lamb	Exodus 12:21–27
His blood would be spilt	Leviticus 17:11
He will carry the Sceptre out of Israel	Balaam: Numbers 24:17
He is heir to David's Eternal Kingdom	2 Sam. 7:12–13, Daniel 7:13–14
Messiah will die, yet live!	Job 19:25–27 Psalm 118:17–18
He would be forsaken	Psalms 22:1, 31:9–10
He would be crucified!	Psalm 22:16
Messiah would be a sacrifice for sin	Psalm 40:6 – 8
He would speak in parables	Psalm 78:1 – 2
He would be the "Rejected Cornerstone"	Psalm 118:22 – 24
Messiah's name will be *Immanuel*—God with us	Isaiah 7:14
He would commence his ministry in Galilee	Isaiah 9:1 – 2
He would live again!	Isaiah 25:7 – 8
He would be a man of miracles	Isaiah 35:5 – 6
He would be preceded by the forerunner	Isaiah 40:3–4, Mal. 4: 5–6
He would pour out his Spirit	Isaiah 44:3
Messiah would be despised and rejected	Isaiah 53:3
He would bring in a new Covenant	Jeremiah 31:31
He would be the answer—the Atonement—for sin	Daniel 9:24
Messiah would be born in Bethlehem	Micah 5:2
He would ride in peace, on a donkey into Jerusalem	Zechariah 9:9
He would be betrayed	Zechariah 11:12–13
The nation would be sorry and be cleansed	Zechariah 12:10–13:2

I felt in need of giving hope, of offering *shalom* peace after the statements recorded in Zechariah were set down on the wall, now almost blackened by the coal. 'Let us turn our minds again to Isaiah, "the prince of prophets". Listen well to what he foretells:

*The redeemed shall walk the streets of Jerusalem! The ransomed shall return…
gladness and joy will overtake them. Sorrow and weeping will depart!*

'WHY? Take special note of what it is that *YHVH* is saying here:

*Be comforted! My people… Your sins have been paid for! A voice will be
heard crying in the wilderness: 'Prepare the way of the Lord… The glory
of the LORD will be revealed. All nations will see it, will be drawn to it!
I AM, the LORD, has spoken it!*
'And, class, Isaiah has not completed his Good News:
*After his suffering, My righteous servant will see life [again] and be satisfied
because he will bear the sin of humankind. Therefore, his greatness will be known
because he gave his life, numbered together with sinners, pleading their cause…
Let the wicked forsake his way… Let him return to the LORD for He, in
His mercy, will pardon you.*
*Give ear to Me. Hear what I say so that your soul may live! I will make an
everlasting covenant with you… Nations will hasten to you… Mine are
not empty words, they will achieve My purposes.*
*You will walk in joy and peace for, instead of thorns the myrtle trees will
flourish: let this be an everlasting sign that will never be destroyed!*
*Let justice continue by doing what is right because My salvation is close at
hand and My righteousness will soon be revealed to you!*
(Selected verses from Isaiah 35, 40, 53, 55, 56).

Though exhausted, this "part-time rabbi" left the class in some
semblance of order. At least, I felt, we'd gained some ground. In fact,
the would-be teacher felt that he (that is, myself) had gained some solid
ground! There were aspects of our reading and recording of the Isaiah
scroll that had placed some of my erstwhile quandaries on to solid rock!

The thought of Jesus came unbidden, then, to me. Could I see, in
him, the answer to the squalls of fear and fancy that fill the mind when
seeking to address the age-old questions: What? When? Where? How?

Why? Are we yet to see the *Mashiach* (Messiah) in our day? I think, perhaps, we can!

What was particularly pleasing to me was that a new student by the name of David *ben* Manaen had now entered the Temple Rabbinic School! The lad sat quietly enough (was careful to be on his best behaviour for his proud parent, I assumed). There was one morning, though, when the visiting "professor" was surprised to find his son loaded up with some arrows in his quiver! I had been given the subject of "A Minor Prophet and his Contribution to the Faith of our Fathers".

I thought it best to start at the beginning (alphabetically, that is), so Amos, the part-time shepherd-cum-orchardist from Tekoa was the chosen subject. (I knew Tekoa well as it is situated just six miles south of Bethlehem).

The introduction completed, I was about to "launch out into the deep" when, 'Excuse me, *Abba*, oh, I'm sorry, Rabbi, if Amos was from the south, why did he need to go north to present his prophecies?'

I turned the question over to the class. The answer was simple enough. 'Because *YHVH* needed the people in the north to hear the prophecy, Rabbi?' 'Well said, Nathan!' 'But why was Amos the man for the moment?' David inquired.

'David, lad, what has a shepherd learned to do?' 'Well, to take care of his sheep, *Abba*.' 'And what has an orchardist learned to do?

'Dig out the dead wood, plough the ground, prune the trees, harvest the crop... Oh, I see it now. Thanks, *Abba*, ah, Rabbi.'

'Yes, son, hence Amos' reason for speaking of a basket of fruit (Amos 8). Amos needed to proclaim that the time was ripe for the "harvesting" of Israel—not a happy harvest, as history attests! But the orchardist must also prepare for the onslaught of locusts. Amos would have found it so very difficult to proclaim that prophecy—coming as he did from the prosperous south.

'We get ahead of ourselves! The prophecy of Amos begins with a shepherd and his flock—not a happy circumstance as it so happens! The pastures are depleted. The grass has dried up for famine has struck the land. Why?' The answers came thick and fast. This class had already learned to discern the consequence of circumstance. Turn from the One who offers life: spiritual famine and eventual death is the end of it!

'What is the end of things for the Northern Kingdom, um, Rabbi?' 'GOOD news, David; GOOD news, class! *YHVH* says, *I will restore the broken-down tent of King David! I will repair the broken places, rebuild the ruins. Israel shall be restored to its former glory!*

'Also, the Holy Text reads: *Israel will be replanted in their own 'orchard' never to be uprooted again. This is the word of the LORD!* (Amos 9).

The way was now open for spirited discussion on the charcoal headings that I swiftly applied to the wall:

REDEMPTION ... RESTORATION ...RENEWAL ... RIGHTEOUSNESS

'So! Class, how are we to be good shepherds? Answers were written in charcoal:

CARE
GUIDANCE
EN FOLD ING
PROVIDE PASTURE
THE SHEPHERD'S PSALM!

'The lesson is not complete until we place ourselves in the role of the orchardist. Take the charcoal, David: be our scribe! How are we to be good orchardists?'

DIG OUT THE DEAD WOOD
PRUNE UNRULY GROWTH
TEND THE MATURING CROP
HARVEST GOOD FRUIT

It was time for affirmation and for prayer!

I returned home at the end of the day with a deep sense of relief. My dearly loved son was shaping up most satisfactorily among his class mates. It was a joy to behold

12. LANDSCAPES AND SEASCAPES

'What? What's that you say? The desert man, John the baptiser, thrown into prison? Why? Maryam, why? 'My dear, it's because of the present palace intrigues. My brother, Antipas, was enraged for John had dared to condemn him because of his so-called marriage to his sister-in-law—Herodias—Philip's wife! The baptiser challenged Antipas with, "It is not lawful for you to take her from your brother!" He is right, though. Antipas wants to kill John but I do not think he will for he is afraid of a backlash from the people.'

'It's not hard to get them all mixed up. Antipas is the son of Herod the Great and Malthace. Philip is also Herod's son though his mother was Mariamne. Philip lives in Rome. He married Herodias, who is actually his niece. Antipas was visiting the couple when he persuaded Herodias to forsake her husband for him (another uncle). Such a travesty of decency is forbidden in The Law! John, the baptiser, was right to condemn him. The question is, will Antipas ever relent and release him? A guilty conscience can make matters worse for a king or a commoner if the knees are weak!' 'We can only hope for the best.'

'Maryam, I'm home early today for I'm to be on the road again! I am to journey north to the Galilee region. People are gossiping about the one they call "The Nazarene". Nicodemus has instructed me to investigate the situation to get the stories in perspective. Maryam, I am of a mind to say that the subject of my search is none other than *Yeshua*—Jesus! You see, in the early prophecies of Isaiah there is a simply magnificent promise:

In Galilee of the Gentiles, the people living in darkness have seen a great light; upon those living in the land of the shadow of death, this light has dawned. (Isaiah 9:2).

'Maryam, a "Light" is dawning in me! I have my doubts but I am finding that my hopes are growing stronger. Perhaps, among "the Gentile world" I will realise my faith! I'll hurry back to you as soon as I am able. Come, let's linger in our room tonight.'

The journey north was extremely arduous. I had not trekked this way before and it was difficult to determine the route I should take. I had decided to travel up into the hill country to the west of the great lake. Arriving in Nazareth, I sought lodging. I arose quite refreshed and following a nourishing meal, went in search of the carpenter's shop!

I was too late! The carpenter of Nazareth had already departed from his home town. I was told that he was stirring up the populace in Capernaum, a flourishing fishing village on the shores of Lake Galilee. But the journey to the hills had been worthwhile. I found her there! Mary, the mother of Jesus, our neighbours for that year or so in Bethlehem! Because they had journeyed from this town of Nazareth all that way southward to Bethlehem (I now knew how hazardous this was), I had found my friend, *kebaa-baa-baas...* "The Lamb... of God"? Is he the one who would conquer sin? I had a need to know!

114

My time with Mary, Jesus' mother, was so very beneficial. The silent years were filled in capaciously and I felt that now "The Nazarene" was more fully known to me. Joseph had died many years ago and Jesus—as the eldest son—took on the responsibility of managing both home and business until he reached the age of thirty. Now his nearest sibling, James, had taken over this role. Mary was yet quite well and would journey down to Capernaum occasionally. As for me, I must take to the road without further delay. I left the town of Nazareth with some regret. There was a vibrant community housed in those hills.

Surprising, really, how quickly one can reach a destination when the anticipation of meeting a friend is in the offing! My first view of Lake Galilee up close was at Tiberius—a modern town, built up by the emperor of that name. I found it most hospitable.

The following morning, I hiked up to Capernaum which was situated on the northern shores of the lake. The journey is not an extensive one and I found the scenery to be uplifting, rejuvenating! Capernaum is such a surprising place. The synagogue dominates the village. The structure is quite exceptional.

As I moved about this bustling township, I became aware that people were out and about for more reasons than the need to ensure the food safes were replenished adequately. What could it be?

One is drawn to the water's edge. Looking southward, it is immediately acknowledged that the lake could also be known as the Sea of Galilee as the expanse is wide and long and obviously very deep.

I've since learned that fierce squalls can rise without warning to turn the tranquil to the turbulent. Such was not the case that first of days by Galilee. I took the opportunity to sit upon a rocky outcrop and allow my tired, soiled, un-sandaled feet to wallow in the refreshing shallows.

It was then that I saw him! No doubts. The stance was unique. Commanding yet kindly, warm and welcoming: Jesus! My friend! He was calling to some men who were dealing with their nets aboard a small but sturdy boat. It appeared that their haul of fish was substantial. I watched them at work but was suddenly arrested by the confident call.

(Reminiscent, in part, of a painting by F. R. Petrie)

They left their nets then, those men. An older man was left holding the tiller as the youngsters hurried through the water to the man I knew as Jesus now, waiting for them to come to his side. I learned to know these men! They would be at his side through thick and thin, sun or thunder storms—there were to be plenty of those—from that day on. I was near enough to hear his call: *Come, leave your nets and all those fish! I will make you to become fishers of people. Will you come with me?*

I wished then that I could have left my writing kit to go with him—to the end of the Earth, if necessary! Not possible, of course. There was Maryam and David. I must care for them. But could I enable our David *to become the best that he could be?*

I set about the work in hand. There were people to interview. Much lay ahead of me. It was thought most appropriate that I should first investigate the many instances where people were claiming to have been made well. Many, sick in body for many years, others, sick at heart. No matter the ailment, the results were incredible: instantaneous, illogical! There could be no gainsaying of the readily forth-coming testimonies. I recorded the many testimonies via "the poet's pen"!

THE MIRACLES

He touched my eyes, by faith I see!
New insights are God's gifts to me
As he reveals Eternity!
This is a mighty miracle.

He touched my lips, now I can speak
Of how he lifted me from woe;
Through grace this is faith's mountain peak:
Oh yes, this is a miracle!

He touched my mind and now I know
His calm can permeate the soul.
In grief, he shall his peace bestow;
I find this is a miracle!

He touched my heart, my soul is freed
From depths of night to paths of light!
And day by day my Lord will lead;

For me, this is a miracle!

He touched my life, I am made whole,
He took my hand and lifted me;
A new dawn breaks upon my soul;
This is a wondrous miracle.

The following day required a hike to the hills at the north of the lake. The view was splendiferous! I would pause occasionally to take in the beauty of these surroundings. But there was need to hurry on as it appeared the whole village was bent on following the Galilean rabbi as he ascended to what was a natural amphitheatre—ideal for the purpose of his teaching ministry. How fortunate I was to have brought my writing kit with me. I was able, again in the mode of poetry, to encapsulate a day's teaching on my hastily prepared parchment.

THE BEATITUDES

'How blessed you are,' the rabbi said:
'You're Heaven's child! Though poor you are,
You're rich! Within your soul be glad;
In God's own Kingdom you will share!'

'How blessed you are!' The rabbi knew
That those who mourn may find his peace!
'He'll comfort you, accompany you;
From deepest grief, he'll bring release!'

'How blessed you are,' the rabbi cried,
'The meek are held by grace and love;
The hungry will be satisfied,
My Father's giving you will prove!'

'How blessed you are!' The rabbi's word:

119

'The merciful, God's mercy still,
The pure in heart will see the LORD,
The peaceful? Peace their heart will fill.

'How blessed you are!' The rabbi said:
'When persecuted for your faith:
Look unto God for He has dared
To lead you in His Kingdom path!'

'How blessed you are, the victory's won!
Rejoice with all your heart and soul.
Your Heavenly recompense is known:
Through Him, the Lord, you are made whole!'

Jesus, as a rabbi, was invited to share his insights in the local synagogue. He read from The Law and the Prophets but I was discovering that this man, this unique rabbi, was actually demanding more of the populace than The Law demanded. Amazing, radical!

I had never heard The Law applied in this revolutionary way. Yet I had to affirm, in my own way, that not a word was out of place. Jesus was giving a new understanding of The Law—in effect, bringing The Law to the people rather than the people to The Law and in a way that they were hungry to hear more and respond most readily to his teaching. What a rabbi I have found! Nicodemus would be made aware of it!

Repeatedly I would hear him declare: 'You know how The Law says... But I say to you...' For example, I caught hold of the following:

'You have heard it said, An eye for an eye and a tooth for a tooth. But I say to you: Do not resist evil people. If someone strikes you in the face with his fist, present the other cheek to him! If someone takes your tunic, offer your cloak as well. Love your enemies, do good to those that harm you so that it may truly be said of you that you are a son, a daughter of God. If you love just those who love you but hate those who do you harm, what good does that bring to you, or them? What are you doing to be different and to make a difference in the lives of others? Endeavour to live without blame. Then you will be emulating the qualities that your heavenly Father imparts. You can become what you are meant to be!

Jesus said much about prayer and it took me all my time to record as much as possible of his innovative approach to prayer. He provided a pattern that is second to none in his approach to communion with his Father in Heaven. He prefaced his remarks by a few humorous comments:

There's no need to keep babbling on as if YHVH is away in a far country and will take time to respond to you. Such folk think that He will hear them if they keep prattling on for long enough. There's no need for that! Your Heavenly Father knows what you need before you ask. He is happy when you bring your needs, your joys, your distress, your time to Him! Lay out your requests simply before Him. He will respond!

In order to give you the pattern that Jesus gave to the people in Capernaum and surrounding districts, I will resort to poetry once more:

THE LORD'S PRAYER

Lord, we would learn to simply pray;
How may we worship You?
How shall we speak, what can we say?
Lord, teach us how to pray.

Pray now: 'Father, come what may,
We hallow Your great Name;
LORD, may Your Kingdom come to stay,
Your will be done on Earth.

Provide our food from Your own hand,
Grant us our daily bread;
We give You thanks for You sustain
Our lives from day to day.

Forgive us for our sins, O LORD:
Wrongs done, or good undone,
For we would seek the ways of God,
Forgiving others here.

LORD, keep us from temptation's claim,
Free us from evil's power;
O LORD, we call upon Your Name,
We seek Your aid today.

We worship and adore you, LORD,
Rule in our hearts, we pray;
We will Your power and glory laud
And hail Your Kingdom reign.'

A ground-breaking moment came for me as I, the visiting, inquisitive scribe, joined with a gathering crowd. The local centurion—well respected by the community, I noted—approached Jesus in the street. 'Rabbi, my servant is in agony. He lies paralysed in my home; will you help?' 'I'll come at once!' 'No, Rabbi, I'm not worthy for you to come to us; just speak your healing words and he shall be healed!' 'Go then, you will find that your servant is now well!' Turning to the crowd, Jesus said, 'I have never seen faith such as this centurion's in all Israel!'

A lasting memory of those dramatic, radical, yet wonderfully fulfilling days in the environs of Capernaum was that unforgettable scene of Jesus sitting with the children whose parents had requested him to bless.

The days assigned to me for the Galilean Inspection of "The Nazarene" were demanding, yes, but in so many ways, it was a life-enriching experience. There were occasions when I could lay aside my writing kit to share some brief respite with Jesus and also with those eager young men who he'd chosen to assist him in his work.

Simon appeared to me to be a born leader! Andrew, his brother, more reserved yet so effective in introducing people to the rabbi. Then, the sons of Zebedee. What a pair they were. Already they had gained a reputation and resultant "title" attached to them: "The sons of thunder"! I came to know them as James and John, the latter with a depth of mind that would surprise the wise! These men were students, *disciples*, but already well-versed in The Law! They would make their mark when fully trained by the master teacher: Jesus!

It was time to roll up my parchment, don my travelling robes and make my way southward to Jerusalem… to Maryam… to David… to Nicodemus. I had much to share with them! Oh, to see their dear faces once again. Is all well with them? I longed to know.

13. PROBLEMS AT THE PALACE

'Must we?' I wanted my unambiguous reticence to be heard by Maryam. 'Must we go to the palace?' I was disturbed by the very thought of it. 'Maryam, you are aware that Antipas finds it difficult to be civil with me. I really think that it has to do with my friendship with "The Nazarene". I have concerns about where all that will lead.' 'My dear, the occasion is a banquet. There will be no need to associate with him. We can sit at a far table and please ourselves instead of my brother!'

It was settled, then. We would present ourselves at the palace and partake of exotic niceties but confine ourselves to conversations with some more kindly couples who would gather to celebrate the royal event. Granted, the meal was scrumptious. There were some friends at our table so all was acceptable until… until… the princess Salome came drifting in with flowing robes to dance her wants and wiles!

The disrobing was revolting. The ogling was quite lurid and, as the last of Salome's veils fell from her lithesome form, applause broke out. 'Maryam, I think it's time we left.' 'Yes, we must. But wait, what's that my brother says?' 'Do it again, [hic] Salome, present your dance again! Yes, [hic] again! You request a gift [hic] my dear? Anything! I'd give the half of [hic] my kingdom to see you tell of your [hic] desires in that dance! What is it that would [hic] suffice for you, my dear?'

'Mother, please tell me, what should I ask of Herod now?' 'Salome, my child, ask for the head of the Baptist! He's rankled me enough. How dare he point the finger at my marriage to Antipas! Yes! Off with the Baptist's head!'

It must be said that, even in his drunken state, Herod was appalled! 'Not that, [hic] Salome! Not that!' But Herod thought again. He'd made a promise to the princess. He could not renege on that. There were people looking on, listening. He must keep his word! So, if the head was to be the payment for that dance of the flowing veils, then payment it would be. 'Off with the Baptist's [hic] head!'

As Maryam and I rose to leave all this horrific debauchery, the door opened and a slave entered, carrying a large salver dripping with the blood still oozing from the severed head of John the Baptist. 'Maryam, I will never, but never enter this palace again. As that head is severed, I now sever my connection to Herod Antipas! I do not ask of you the same—he is your brother yet.' 'Manaen, I am with you, I leave with you, I stay with you and I agree with you!'

Sometime after that ghastly event, Nicodemus informed me that a group of his friends—Pharisees, in fact—had approached Jesus with some disquieting news. 'Rabbi, you must leave Jerusalem. Herod Antipas means to kill you!'

They had been given an unequivocal reply: 'You go back to that fox and tell him this: I will continue my ministry today, tomorrow and the day after. On the third day I will reach my goal. And, besides, no prophet dies outside of Jerusalem!'

Nicodemus continued the report of his exchange with his friendly Pharisees. 'Manaen, my informants went on to tell me about a grief that Jesus verbalised. I fear its consequence! It was a plea, a prayer and a pronouncement:

Oh Jerusalem, you kill the prophets, you stone those sent to you. But I have longed to gather you up in in my arms—like a hen gathers her chicks but you would not come to me. Your "house" will be left desolate.'

'Nicodemus, you know that Jesus of Nazareth has promised to visit me while in Jerusalem. Would you be willing to come for an evening meal and meet with him? I am aware that there are questions in your mind that lie still unresolved, questions that I share with you.

'We've talked of the person and presence of the *ruach*, the Holy Spirit. I'm sure that you need only ask the question and he will elucidate the answer out of his own great storehouse of wisdom! Will you come? You will? I will make arrangements for the meeting to take place as soon as he is able.'

The arrangements for this very special meal were meticulous and Maryam's cooking was superb—as always, I must admit. Fish was the major item on the menu. We could hardly wait for his arrival!

Jesus came to us, he sat with us! The conversation flowed quite flawlessly! At times, Jesus would question us. At times, our questions were for him! There was give and take. The answers were a blessing to our souls! We hoped that he'd be pleased with our response to his own questioning.

He came! Nicodemus broached the subject dear to his questing heart. 'Rabbi, we are aware that your ministry is of the LORD—it would be impossible to do what you are doing unless the LORD is working through you. We believe that the Kingdom of God will come because of your work among us.' Jesus surprised him and us as well as he replied, 'No one will even see the Kingdom of God unless he or she is born again!'

'How can that be possible? How could a man be born again if he is already a mature man? He couldn't possibly return to his mother's womb to perform a second exit?!' 'I am telling you the truth. One may enter the kingdom of God only by experiencing two births!' 'Two births?' 'Rabbi, what can you mean?' 'The first birth is the physical birth—that of the water. The second birth is the spiritual birth! Flesh gives birth to flesh but it is the Holy Spirit who gives birth to the spirit. Why are you so surprised by my statement that one must be "born again"?

'Think of the wind, Nicodemus. It blows where it will. You can hear it, you can see its effects—sometimes gentle, other times rustling, rushing. You cannot tell from whence it comes nor where it will go. In just this way, one is "born of the Spirit".' 'But how, Rabbi? How?' 'Nicodemus! You are Israel's premier teacher and you cannot explain this simple thing? If you cannot understand simple parables, how will you be able to explain spiritual matters? People don't go up to Heaven to discover spiritual truth. It required "the Son of Man" to come down to meet with humanity where they are.

'Nicodemus, I will now speak another parable to you that I know you will understand: Moses presented a symbol of how the LORD will deal with sin. He raised up a serpent on a pole in the wilderness. Everyone who looked to that symbol was able to live! In just the same way the Son of Man must be "lifted up" so that all who believe in him will be saved! You see, God so loves this world that He gives His only Son that whoever will believe in Him shall not perish but have Eternal Life! God has not sent His Son into the world to condemn the world. On the contrary, it is His desire that the world will be saved. (See John 3).

'You ask what is the problem? It's this: light has come into the world; it is shining, it is life-giving, but people love the darkness rather than the light because their deeds are evil. How does one find the light? Live by the truth, Nicodemus, the truth will set you free!' (See John 8).

Magnificent! We were left speechless by the powerful impact of Jesus' words. The shock of the evening was the inference that "the Son of Man" (obviously, the Messiah) would be lifted up on a pole that others might live. He spoke of that desert happening as being symbolic. Symbols point to reality. The Messiah? On a pole?

We turned from that disconcerting parable to the illustration of the wind. This certainly gave us much food for thought. We may discern the coming of the Holy Spirit, we may experience the effect but we can never comprehend fully the movement of the Spirit in our lives. When our visitors had left, Maryam retired for the night but I took up my writing kit. The Spirit "Wind" must be addressed:

THE RUSTLING WIND

Oh, listen for the wind,
It stirs the fragile grass,
It ripples on the restless waves,
The clouds will trace its paths.
Just so, the Spirit stirs
The human soul to life
Inspiring us to trust in God,
Infusing faith's belief.

Oh, listen to the wind,
From whence it comes or goes;
No one can ever choose its ways
Nor tell of where it flows.
Just so, the Spirit-breath
Will move deep in the soul
Investing life with blessed hope,
Inviting to be whole.

Oh, listen in the wind!
The rustling, gale-swept trees
Reveal its presence in the leaves
As nature stirs the breeze.
Just so, the Spirit's power
Encourages the soul

Infusing inner fortitude,
Increasing power to all.

Oh, Listen! Here's the wind;
Now hear its lilting voice;
It whispers on its wending way,
It bids us to rejoice.
Just so, the Spirit's course
Will guide us and sustain,
Invigorating every aim
Immortal life to gain.
(Choir: D.S.M. e.g. *Diademata*)

The evening had been a game changer, a life-changer! But there are major issues to be considered! I have known Jesus to be "the lamb"! I had discovered him to be a rabbi of unique capacity. There was a disturbing hint that he could actually be "the Messiah". Tonight, however, Jesus gave even stronger indicators as to his true identity. He spoke of "The Son of Man". I had not encountered that title since rabbinic school when studying the messages of the prophets—Ezekiel, for example.

The most astounding declaration of all, forever, was that Jesus spoke of being the "Son of God"! How could we come to terms with this amazing, disturbing, contentious declaration? Oh yes, there were yet many unanswered questions!

Word on the street was that the rabbi from obscurity—the north— was treading on thin ice! He was unafraid of the consequences of his denunciation of the "whitewashed sepulchres".

Someone needed to inform him that his days were numbered if he continued to point his finger at our ecclesiastical "heads of state"! I was delegated, of course, to inspect and report. I found myself to be immersed in matters beyond my ken! There were, however, some disturbing thoughts of my own evolving in the meantime.

Assessments were gelling in my mind that related to the true condition of the Community of Faith—a term that gave me ground to determine a perceived difference between genuine followers of the LORD, living out their faith in word and deed, and those who wore the cloak of goodness while, in their heart, far from God!

My musing took me on a virtual "journey" down the far future where the ecclesia, wearing cloaks of a different ilk, could find itself buried by its own spade if not heedful of the truth that cloaks do not make the man. As Samuel of old declared, *Humankind looks upon the outward appearance but God observes the inner life: the heart!*

Following this line of reasoning, I began to record some disturbing assessments that relate not only to Today but also Tomorrow, the face of which I do not see so have no way of determining its future circumstance. It may be, I considered, that my thoughts are meant to make me sit up and take notice. If the heart (the soul) is not functioning as God ordained, the outward trappings are of dubious consequence!

Where are the outward trappings most noticeable from my viewpoint? I walk each day through the courtyards of the Temple on the way to dispatch my scribblings and realise that much of what is "washed white" even in this hallowed place could cover up a shady sham!

Who am I to speak of future days? Sufficient for the day is its evil! Let the future take good care of itself! On second thoughts, Jesus' description of surface saints—"whitewashed sepulchres"—may be meant as a warning not only for Today but also, Tomorrow!

What do I mean? Where is my writing kit? Ah, there! I began to see the dangers, the warnings, the "whitewash"!

WHITEWASHED SEPULCHRES

Religion replacing Righteousness
Ritual replacing Reason
Rigidity replacing Release
Rote replacing Reality
Repine replacing Repose
Ranting replacing Reassurance

Rebuke replacing Rebirth
Renunciation replacing Reconciliation
Regime replacing Redemption
Remonstrance replacing Rejoicing

I put down my writing tool, having come to a significant realisation of what the cloaks of commitment may convey. "Whitewashed sepulchres" are those that are presented *whole and holy* by a cover-up cloak that obscures a putrid, cancerous growth! My conviction solidified: *WE NEED YESHUA–JESUS AS OUR SAVIOUR!*

The outcome of my musing brought me to the conclusion that, if the "sepulchre" is spruced up by a new coat of paint, it is DEATH that lies under the whitewash of pseudo purity. These thoughts did not encourage me! Did I need a new "coat of paint"? A new cloak? Or did I need some change, some cleansing, to take place within my own inner life? I went to my mentor. 'Nicodemus, I need some advice'. 'Don't come to me, Manaen: I also need some advice! Come with me to "The Nazarene"!

'Friends, I didn't come to destroy, to abolish, The Law or the Prophets! I came that their inherent truth may be fulfilled! I can assure you that, until the very end of time, not even the smallest letter ׳ (*yod*) nor even the most minute stroke as part of a letter—look at the tittle to the right side of the base of ב (*bayith*) to get my meaning—would be erased until everything that *YHVH* has ordained is accomplished! The vital thing for you to know is that, if your righteousness does not surpass what the Pharisees and yes, the lawyers teach, it will not be possible to enter the Kingdom of God!'

'How do we gain that which *YHVH* longs to give to us?' 'Ask! It will be given to you! Seek after what He longs to give and you will find it. Knock and the door of God's grace will be opened to you! Would you think that, in asking for bread, *YHVH* would fill your hands with stones? Let me sum up for you—in one simple sentence—the entire content of The Law and the Prophets: *Do to others what you would like them to do for you!* In other words: Love God, and do what you like!'

'Do what we like, Rabbi? Do what we like?' 'Dear friends, if you truly love your Father in Heaven, what you will really like to do is love Him and to be kind and loving to others—your enemies as well as your neighbours. You will enjoy doing for others what you long to have happen for you! The entirety of The Law and The Prophets rests on that simple statement. Go! Do what you like to do. My Father will smile on you!'

When discussing this radical attitude toward The Law upon our return to the Hall of Hewn Stones, I ventured to say, 'Nicodemus, I feel that I am for him but not yet with him. Is there hope for me?' 'What is your problem, Manaen?' 'It's Maryam. I must continue to include her in my life. I do not want to walk away from her. And David, he will not be helped right now by a vacillating parent.' 'An excellent sentiment, Manaen. But why not invite them to also walk the path that you are beginning to tread?'

'Your outlook and your attitude to life brings such encouragement to me. I'm of the opinion, Nicodemus, that "The Wind" is now in your "sails". But where are you going, Nicodemus? What is your destination?' 'Ah! Manaen, I see that you also took to heart the parable of "The Wind". Allow the *ruach*, "Wind", of God to also fill your "sails"!' 'I will apply my heart to it,' I replied.

'Nicodemus, how will you approach the Sanhedrin now that your outlook and in-look on life has undergone such a significant change?' 'Manaen, for better or for worse, I have determined to keep my allegiance to Jesus to myself. I'm of the opinion that to stand up for him vocally would be like throwing him and me to the wolves, so to speak. 'Perhaps it is better than I fight for him without the verbiage yet. I will apply his principles whenever I can but—at present—I must follow the letter of The Law for the sake of the Sanhedrin and the status quo, I guess! I suppose that I am nothing but a silent ambassador. Of what good is that? You may well ask. What this will do for him I do not know. But, if and when the test does come, I am his man!' It seemed to me that Nicodemus was walking a tight rope more tenuous than mine!

The ministry of Jesus continued on apace. He and his disciples traversed the land. Disciples! Why do so many hear the word *discipline* with such negativity? It seems to me that the word is now thought to describe a verbal onslaught, a physical retribution, rather than the opportunity given to be schooled in right attitudes and behaviour patterns. Oh, to be taught, mentored, guided, counselled by Jesus of Nazareth! The privileges experienced by his disciples are unrivalled!

I was always pleased when Jesus entered the city. It meant that I could give close attention to his activities, and to his potent proclamations. One day in the Temple, another by the Pool of Bethesda, another on Olivet, then on to Bethany where the siblings— Martha, Mary and Lazarus—had become his adherents. It was my privilege to hear his sometimes gentle, sometimes forceful approach to his teaching ministry.

Just think, if you will, of the impact of Jesus' response to the sheep being herded through the Sheep Gate toward the Outer Court of the Temple. These sheep were due for a slaughter that would atone for the sins of the nation. Here was "The Lamb of God" observing the many, many lambs accounted as being without blemish in order to be accounted fit for slaughtering. He turned my gaze from the *kebes* to the carers and declared: *I AM the Good Shepherd. I will give my life for the sheep.* Not now, "The Lamb" being led to the slaughter, it is the Shepherd who will surrender his life for the lambs, the sheep!

My son was causing me some disquiet: young David—of the Tribe of Judah—therefore more royal in fact than Antipas, the Prince from Edom's stock! Outgrowing his playtime game of being a "half-prince", David had been influenced by a close-knit group of students at the Rabbinic School. He and his friends were becoming engrossed in the comings and the goings of the party known as the Zealots.

David had become adamant in his attitudes. His ideas were sound enough: The Law was sacrosanct, but the Zealots had developed rancorous ways of proclaiming their principles! My fear for him stemmed from his emboldened activities, bent on bringing about revolutionary change. A more mature mind could see plainly what the only possible outcome would be! We could lose our son!

How does one deal with such a dilemma? Just one parent dealing with the problem was more likely to fail. It required both parents to focus on their son. How best to counsel him? How best to *disciple* the lad? These were difficult days and the invasion of "The Nazarene" into our city streets did in no way ease the situation. The boy could see that I was grappling with the burden of balancing The Law with Grace. Is *YHVH* the God of vengeance or the God of loving-kindness? Where does one draw the line? How does one bring a definitive answer to the questing of our child, our boy, our young man, our SON! '*Eloi, Eloi*, please: grant us guidance, help us to advise our son effectively.'

I saw Jesus yet again immersed in his healing ministry. Wonderful results! There was a cripple who had mostly lived, for almost forty years, sheltered by the colonnades at the Pool of Bethesda with no one caring to assist him into the "healing" pool—till Jesus walked that way. The man was invited to pick up his bed and walk! He took Jesus at his word. He stood up, rolled up his mat and walked. The thing that really touched a nerve in me was that the man was then accosted by some of my contemporaries. 'Don't you realise that it is the *sabbath*? The Law forbids anyone to carry a burden today?' 'The man who healed me told me to pick up my bedding and begin to walk. That's what I am doing! I am going to the Temple now to thank God for this miracle. No, I don't know the healer's name.' He did discover it, then told the authorities.

The thing is, I should have stepped right in to correct the error being made at the pool. The Law does not, in fact, state that it is forbidden to carry a burden on the *sabbath*. It is the interpretation of The Law that makes life so very difficult by the multitudinous interpolations, the endless "refinements", added to the Holy Writ! I should speak up!

There was another, similar instance. A man that had been blind from his birth had met with Jesus. The rabbi healed the man!

(Based on a statue near Galilee)

Just think of it! Who could believe it? Jesus plastered the man's eyes with mud made from his spit! He then instructed that the man be taken to the Pool of Siloam for cleansing. He went. He washed the mud from his eyes. He could see. For the first time in his life, he could see!

The man's view soon turned from grace to that of grief for he was accosted by a group of my associates who exclaimed that the healer was not of God! He worked on *sabbath*! I did step in on this occasion—with a barbed question for the inquisitors: 'How is it that a sinner can bring about such a miracle as a blind man—who had never seen—being given his sight?' That set them on their heels. But they regained their "footing" and exclaimed, 'We know this man is a sinner!'

Joy! Oh joy! To have been there! To have heard the man's unequivocal answer. It was an utter delight to me! 'Whether he is a sinner or not, I do not know. But there is one thing that I do know: once I was blind and now, I'm not! All my life, blind. But for the rest of my life, I will be able to see! HALLELUJAH!'

14. A DONKEY-RIDE FROM OLIVET

'David, come and walk with me. You and I need a "man-to-man" today. You're a grown man now and I? Fairly elderly and grey! But we are "one". You are bone of my bone and flesh of my flesh. It's time we spoke of more than, 'How has your day been? Are you tired? What happened to rile your blood today? Let's walk awhile, chat awhile.

'You know, my lad, that your Mother and I have some fear for your on-going safety. It's not just the usual parental problems that break into our happiness for you apply yourself so heartily to your well-defined aims and aspirations. The fact is, son, there are clouds gathering over "The City of David". We know that you love Jerusalem and would give your all to ensure that, one day, it can rightly be called "The City of Peace". David, how will you activate the aims that are forming in your soul?'

'*Abbi*, why are you afraid for me? I see no harm in voicing my opinions whenever I see our people bowing to all the wants and wishes of the Roman conquerors! We should be no longer subservient, bowing and scraping before their regimented might!'

'Come, David, let's go through the East Gate and on down into the valley where the Kidron flows. We can sit a while and ponder how the river's flow can speak to us both.'

'So, here we are, nicely settled by the brook. Do you know why this stream gained its name, David?' 'Oh yes, *abbi*. It is the *turbid* stream: muddy, murky, troubled, turbulent or, sometimes, dry!' 'That's so, son. But the Kidron has other unfortunate aspects. It rises in the rugged mountains, flows past Jerusalem's Temple—its water is never purified—then on down through the barren mountains to meet its sorry end. Kidron flows into the "Dead Sea"! It's really why I brought you here today. We—both of us—need to heed the message of the Kidron!"

'*Abbi*, I don't get what you mean! How can a muddy stream tell us what we need to know?' 'David, I am aware that your Zealot Party is currently under scrutiny. How committed are you? I hope for you to find the wise way, to tread on safe ground rather than immerse yourself in the muddy waters of a turbulent "stream" that can only end in a "Dead Sea" of wasted ambitions.'

'*Abba*, I can't back off what I firmly believe. I cannot compromise the matters that hold my soul to The Law! That matter of unjust taxes, for example, is gnawing at my peace of mind. We deserve—as *YHVH's* people—to be FREE*!* The spirit of Queen Mariamne stirs my soul! The Hasmonean heritage is bred in me! We need another Judas Maccabee!

'No, no! don't worry so, *abbi*! I am not that man but I will support him when he appears. Too long we've lived in apathy. We can't continue to sit it out. We must do something!'

'David, lad, you are the "prince of my heart"! I do admire your tenacity and your theology—you serve *YHVH* unstintingly—but, please, allow this word of caution: fanaticism that leads to brazen attitudes and actions can end in disaster. Please, bide your time and act only when no other alternative is possible.

'The Zealot Party may need to become more accepting of Gentiles. Your Pharisaic beliefs are shared by my good friend Nicodemus, but he is less likely to be activated to break the yoke of Rome before the time is right, than your Zealots. Please, please, my son, do not allow these troublesome, turbid attitudes to carry you down into a "Dead Sea"!

'Father, I hear what you say and will, comply within reason—as much as is possible. I have no desire to step aside from the aspirations you and Mother hold for me. But, *Abbi*, I must follow the dictates of my soul!'

'David, you look for a "Champion". Have you given careful thought to the teaching of Jesus, the Nazarene? One of his disciples is known as Simon, the Zealot. Jesus sees the good in him, the potential he has to be both zealous and kind! The two aspects can go hand-in-hand!'

'Father, I am waiting for him to declare himself. It may well be that I could follow him. I will make a point of listening carefully to the statements he makes when next he comes to Jerusalem.'

'I say, look at that crowd forming. It looks as if there's some festive occasion I know not of! Would you believe it? There are people ripping palm branches from the trees. It seems that everyone is in a dancing mood.' 'Listen *abbi*! Listen! Everyone is chanting "*Hosanna*".' 'How very strange: *Hosanna* can hardly be the chant of a dance! Come, let's see what the excitement is all about!'

'There he is, David! There he is! It's Jesus and he's riding towards Jerusalem on the back of a donkey! He's about to cross the Kidron! Come close. I'll test you now, my son! What is the Scripture that should come to mind?'

'That's easy *abbi*! Can it be that this Scripture is fulfilled today?'

הנה מלכך יבוא לך צדיק ונושע הוא עני ורכב על–חמור
Behold, your king is coming to you, righteous and victorious.
He is humble and riding on an ass. (Zechariah 9:9)

'Your knowledge of the text is excellent, David! But what is the meaning of הושע–נא?' *'Abba*, they are praying the word but dancing to "another tune!"'

'Well said, *beni* (my son)! Well said! *Hosanna* is the desperate plea of a people needing to be saved, saved *NOW!* It is a plea for help! Yet the chanting of Zechariah's prophecy is a dance for joy! Why? Why such a juxtaposition? These people believe that Jesus of Nazareth *IS* the King who comes to set them free! The scene is wholly in keeping with your sentiments, my son! Shall we chant "HALLELUJAH" along with them?'

We were carried along with the exaltation of the thronging crowds. In the midst of it all, the rider on his donkey remained calm and serene. Here was no rampant, victorious king riding on a white stallion to emphasise his conquering intent. Here was Jesus, coming in peace to the "City of Peace". More likely, his intent was to bring peace into this city that has known no true peace for hundreds of years! Oh, where is my writing kit?

HOSANNA

Hosanna
O save us, Lord,
save even now—
this very day!

We make our plea:
O, don't you see?
We long for you,
Messiah who
will save us from
the yoke of Rome.

Hosanna
O save me, Lord,
save me, I pray—
this very day!

I make my plea:
now come and be
Messiah, King!
In prayer, I sing
of longings keen
and freedom seen!

Hosanna
Ride on, ride on
and victor be,
O Saviour, Lord!

My personal prayer of *Hosanna* had emerged from past history into the heart needs of today. Conquerors had come, conquerors had gone, vanquished to an inevitable oblivion. This rider was different! He had no proud earthly kingdom to claim! He comes in peace—with peace that would usher in the Kingdom of God! Such a peace as this is far removed from the kind of peace that the "world" has to offer! *YHVH El Shaddai* alone could bring peace of heart to this troubled city. It was my earnest prayer that David would seek the *shalom* peace that Jesus alone can give!

Events were moving at a frenetic pace. I sensed an excitement rising in David. I spoke of it to Maryam that same night with a greater sense of ease concerning our son than I had felt for some time. Perhaps, with the coming of the one I now felt quite sure was the Messiah, David would at last make right choices for his life. Our relaxed attitude did not last for long!

15. SKULL FACE HILL

My entry to the Outer Court of the Temple the following morning filled me with dread. I was confronted with a pandemonium never seen before within these hallowed walls. The frenzy stemmed from the area set down for the money changers' tables. You see, it is required that all tainted money be exchanged for money blessed as "holy" by the priests. So, why the kerfuffle? Oh no! It's him! My *kebes*—lamb, cum *raah*—shepherd, the gentle rabbi from obscurity: in a furious frenzy, shouting, denouncing, overturning tables, casting chairs away, and flinging coins to the wind! What has come over him?

'The Scriptures declare that My House shall be a House of Prayer but you have made it a den of robbers! You know the words of Isaiah and Jeremiah! You disregard their prophecies at your peril! You think you are safe. You cannot trust the Temple to keep you immune from retribution if you delight in sin! (See Luke 19:46).

It must be said that, for all his anger, Jesus was in complete control. It appeared as though everyone was so shocked that they could not mount a defence. For all of that, Jesus had stepped over the mark. He would not, could not, rebound from that morning's tirade against Temple customs. This was holy ground—at least so far as the priests, the Pharisees, the Sadducees and the Zealots were concerned. Even as they cowered before his onslaught, the rulers of the people were consolidating their hatred of this upstart from obscurity. How dare he revile against the sanctity of "God's dwelling place on Earth"! He would have to go—by whatever means to rid them of the man!

I have grave fears for what David has made of all this. Would he agree with the Nazarene's pronouncement, or would he be horrified that anyone—including the Nazarene—should "desecrate" the environs of the Temple, the House of *YHVH El Shaddai*?

Jesus and his men left the Temple precincts, choosing to cross the Kidron once more and hike up the slopes of Mount Olivet. But, before one could breathe a sigh of relief, Jesus and his men had returned to the Temple precincts where he proceeded to proclaim the Good News for which he was now becoming quite famous!

This was like flinging a red rag into the face of a bull! The Chief Priests and the lawyers, together with the elders—Nicodemus and I stood among the group with a somewhat daunted attitude—approached Jesus. I was more than concerned to hear the content of the questioning: 'Who gave you the authority to be preaching in this place? Come now, tell us: who gave you this authority?' His answer truly amazed me!

'I will also ask of you a question and, if you can answer it, I will answer you! Tell me: Were the baptisms carried out by John of God or of man?'

They all went into a "holy huddle"! 'If we say, 'Of God', he is bound to ask, 'Why then did you not believe him?' But if we say 'Of man', we could be stoned for the general populace genuinely believes that John was a prophet.' I found I had to smile at the decision reached. 'We have to say that we do not know.'

'That being the case, neither will I tell you by whose authority I am doing these things.'

Much to the chagrin of the Chief Priests and cohorts, Jesus proceeded to tell a potent parable about some wicked tenants to the many people listening. Briefly, his story concerned the owner of a vineyard who rented it to some orchardists and departed on an extended journey. At harvest time, the owner sent a servant to request some of the harvest. The servant was beaten and sent away empty-handed. The same applied to further servants on the same mission. Finally, the owner decided on a better course of action: 'I will send my son whom I love. Surely they will respect him!' As the son approached the orchardists, they considered the situation and came up with a dastardly plan: 'If we kill the son, we shall gain the inheritance!' The deed was done!

'What then will the owner of the vineyard do to those tenants? He will return. He will punish the tenants. He will give the vineyard to others!'

The anger of the Temple men knew no bounds! They knew that the story referred to them! Jesus then asked them, 'What is the meaning of the Psalmist's words (118:22):

The Stone that the builders rejected has become the Cornerstone?
Be careful! That Stone may fall on you!'

From that morning, the lawyers and the chief priests began to investigate just how to arrest Jesus without further ado. They knew that he had "pointed the finger" at them! But, how to silence him? They were frustrated in their plans for they knew full well that the general populace admired him and would retaliate if he was harmed.

And I? I was now caught between the two—my bosses and the people for, although I was gravely concerned, I saw no fault in what Jesus had declared! How could the matter be resolved in my soul? I had felt I was almost there, a "fringe disciple" of the Nazarene.

Now? I was not so sure! And not because I had to give answer to those that breathed down on me from the lofty heights of the Sanhedrin, but because I could not come to terms with that "Tempest in the Temple". I agreed with his sentiments but the Temple is a Holy Place—though, not if it's made unholy by the obvious flouting of The Law by the discrepancies of money not replaced fairly and honestly. The weights, weighed in the balances, were swinging once more towards my friend, the Nazarene. But, what of David now? Could I save my son? Could I save the Nazarene?

I lingered near the group where Jesus continued to speak his words of wisdom to the crowds and also to his inner group of followers. That's where I stood: near Peter, James and John for I felt I knew them reasonably well after my sojourn in the region of Galilee. I was staggered to hear of his prediction that this age may soon be overtaken by another age of a different ilk. What could he mean? I had to know. Nicodemus had given me licence to attend the gatherings, making notes that would be of value to his work as a member of the Sanhedrin.

My *kebes*, Lamb, my *Yeshua*, Jesus, had always spoken "words of life", words which brought a vigour to the soul. I recall that sermon on the mount just to the north of Lake Galilee. There, he brought down blessings on "the flock". Today's teaching has alarmed me beyond measure! How could he even have dreamt of such an unspeakable horror as this proclamation?

'Look around you. Observe the magnificent architecture, the supreme workmanship of this Temple—consecrated once to the worship of *YHVH El Shaddai.* I say to you now that the day will come when not one stone will be left on top of another. This Temple will be utterly destroyed!'

No! No! No! Impossible! This Temple is impregnable! No army would lay a hand on God's house! Then, someone asked, 'Rabbi, when will this eventuate?'

'Do not be deceived: Do not listen to every Jonah, Job, or Jehoshaphat! Many will be led astray. Do not follow them. You will hear of battles, here and there. These events will come to pass. Nation will enter into conflict with nation. Earthquakes, famines and pestilence will strike fear into the heart of all. But, before this, you will suffer much persecution. You will be betrayed. Listen carefully: if you stand firm, you will gain LIFE!

Would it be possible that, in the face of such complete devastation, there could be reason to hope? I thought: 'only if the Messiah stands by our side!' Where is the Messiah?

'People will be overcome with terror beyond description. Great anguish and perplexity will fill the Earth with horror. It will be at this very time that "The Son of Man" will be seen emerging with great glory from the surrounding clouds. When this time eventuates, stand up, lift your heads because your redemption will be very near!'

A terrifying scenario, to say the least of it! I had to ask, 'Rabbi, will all this happen in our lifetime? Can we expect to see all of which you speak come to pass?'

'My friend, do not expect to know the day or hour when "The Son of Man" will return to Earth to claim his Everlasting Kingdom. No one knows that date! However, let this be a clue for you: learn the parable of the fig tree. Do you not know that, when the leaves of this tree begin to form in spring, the embryo of its fruit may also be seen? Learn the signs that the seasons will bring: you will then determine when the time is near!'

Well, I know this much: The season of The Passover is with us now and, before the week is done, the High Priest will enter the Holy of Holies because the Temple and its time-honoured customs still stand! Now, the day is far spent. Maryam will be wondering what has become of me. I wonder what she has cooking on the hobs tonight? I must get on. But, wait: Jesus is coming my way. 'Come, walk with me, Manaen. There is much I want to say to you!' I thought no more of the evening meal with Maryam!

'My disciples and I cross over Kidron each evening for Gethsemane provides a safe and peaceful haven—for the time being. Come to the Kidron with me.' *Kebes*, I came here just a day or so ago with David, my son. We also had much to say to each other. Jesus smiled at me. That smile has captivated my attention from "day one"—rather, "night one" in Bethlehem! 'I am afraid for him, Jesus. He is a devout follower of the Zealot clan! I have tried to counsel him.' 'The zeal of the Zealots is to be commended if it can be brought into balance by kindness, grace and thoughtfulness.' 'The very thing I said to David. I asked him what the *Kidron* may disclose to those who can discern the right from wrong.' 'What did he say?' 'He spoke of the turbid, muddy, troubled waters of the stream.'

'Dear friend, I know you have your doubts about the things I've said and done in recent days but, in your soul, you do remain sincere— desiring what is best for me. You need to know that I will be *crossing the Kidron* before the week is out. There will be much in the way of muddy waters, the many troubles swirling now will bring a flood upon us all. I am wading through turbid waters, Manaen. I ask of you one thing: hold on to the faith you have and allow it to increase. The day will come when you will realise the worth of what I say to you now. Carry it with you—in your writing kit if you feel inclined. My friend, I say to you now: we will meet again. Good night! Sleep well!'

I hurried then to Maryam. She did not smile on me! The meal was cold, matching her demeanour. But the atmosphere began to warm once more when I explained my late arrival home. My dear one looked into my eyes and read what she had always known! We were as one again before the night was done. The dishes were left in the sink as we made up for the lost hours of eventide.

The Eve of Passover required that all preparations were complete before the downing of the sun. As for me? I was on self-imposed duty. It was imperative that I did not miss the events of the night. I was well aware that a *kebes*, lamb, without blemish was being prepared for slaughter on the hallowed altar of sacrifice. Its blood would be spilt upon the *caphah*, cover of the Mercy Seat—the lid of the Ark of Covenant—on the Day of Atonement.

By that one pure lamb, the sins of a nation—accrued against their souls for one whole year—would be forgiven! The blood of the lamb would bring AT-ONE-MENT, reconciliation between humankind and *YHVH El Shaddai*. I cannot but think of "*the Lamb of God that takes away the sin of the world*" as John the Baptist expressed the underlying truth so profoundly. Why had I not realised, before this night, what John was really saying at the Jordan River just on three years ago. So very much has happened since that happy reunion with *Yeshua*–Jesus.

Yes! I see it now! The lamb is but a symbol of a greater sacrifice where the *kebes*, Lamb of God—by the sacrifice of our Kinsman Redeemer—would finally solve the mystery of the symbol by laying his sinless life on the "altar" for the sake of humankind who—in spite of our best efforts—can never solve the catastrophe of sin!

Jesus and his twelve disciples were partaking of the Feast of Passover while I was enduring the long hours of a chilly night in the street quite near the house where they were gathered. It was not until some years had passed that I became aware of the happenings at the table that night. Surprisingly, one of the twelve—Judas Iscariot—I noticed, left the gathering and was moving quickly but surreptitiously through the night. To my chagrin, I noted that he was headed for the house of

Caiaphas, the current High Priest! What could his mission be? I was to find out before the wretched night was done!

Finally, Jesus and his remaining men left the building and headed towards the Temple. Now it was relatively easy to follow the proceedings. I found him there, pointing to the decorations of the grape vine on the edifice of the Temple. I heard him speak:

'Here is an artisan's depiction of a grape vine. My friends—yes, I call you friends—I am the True Vine! My Father is the Gardener. He will prune the Vine to discard any unfruitful branches. But know this, no branch can bear any fruit unless it remains in the Vine. Remain in me and I in you so that much fruit will eventuate. If you remain in me and my words remain in you, you may ask what you will, it will be granted. It will be to the glory of my Father that you bear much fruit.'

At times—in a very special moment—a "vision splendid" will fall into my mind. My inner eyes see Jesus now as "The True Vine":

What's that he said? Ask what you will? It will be granted? How come? Wait a minute… Yes! If one remains joined to the "True Vine", there would never be a request made that would bring dishonour to the Vine! The branch will always remain true to the Vine. It will allow fruit to grow that will remain true to the Vine. I love the analogy.

Ah! They are leaving the Temple precincts. Out through the Gate Beautiful, the group descends the slopes leading to the Kidron. Hmmm. Turbulent waters? Tonight? Surely not. He enters into Gethsemane. Immediately, I see he goes to his knees. He is at prayer.

Returning to the group, he asks his men to pray for him. Jesus? In need of prayer? He asks Peter, James and John to come nearer to his own prayer place. He now seems greatly distressed. His petition is heart-wrenching:

'*Abbi,* Father, if it is possible, please take away this "cup" from me. But if it is not possible, Your will be done. Yes, Father, Your will be done!'

I continue to observe the scene from nearby. Jesus comes back to his disciple friends to find them sound asleep. 'Have you fallen asleep again? You will need to watch and pray lest you fall away when temptation bites!

'Stay awake now, the hour has come! Look "The Son of Man" has been betrayed into evil hands. Rise, let us go to meet them. Here is the man—the man who has lived in the house of his friends—the man who will betray me.'

The man in question is recognised by everyone! There is utter disbelief that anyone could treat a friend in such a dastardly way. Standing in the shadows near the scene, I am also aghast. So! That is why Judas Iscariot was seen slinking off to the House of Caiaphas! His villainy is now surpassed by a further degrading act. It is obvious that he wishes to identify the one who is to be arrested. Judas slouches up to his spiritual leader, to whom he owes his everything, and kisses Jesus on the face! No! I have never witnessed such an infamous betrayal as this—thrown to "the wolves" by a so-called friend.

'Whom do you seek?' Jesus asks of the soldiers gathered round him now. 'Jesus, the Nazarene.' 'I am he! No, Peter! Put that sword away. My Father's will must be fulfilled.' There is blood but the touch of Jesus staunches its flow. The man's ear is healed!

I can do no other than follow Jesus, his disciples and the soldiers as they again cross the Kidron and march their way up the slopes towards the city gate. I now realise what Jesus meant by that enigmatic statement about *crossing the Kidron through troubled waters* just those few days ago!

The march is longer than expected! We have entered the Quarter where the home of Annas is located. The plot thickens! Annas is the father-in-law of Caiaphas—the current High Priest—though most of us have a private query or two about that! Annas had been deposed by the Romans well over a dozen years ago. Caiaphas had taken "the chair". But Annas still claimed that chair as his own and continued—with impunity—to wield his power! Both High Priests would be involved in the dastardly deeds of this night.

The whisper around the Hall of Hewn Stones has it that Caiaphas had pronounced that—if Jesus were taken during the Feast of Passover— it would serve to emphasise that it would be acceptable for one man to die on behalf of the people. In retrospect, I think that he spoke better than he would ever know!

The inquisition commences. Annas begins his diatribe of accusation concerning the subject matter of Jesus' teaching within the Temple Courts and also in the rural synagogues. 'I have spoken openly. I have not sought dark corners to proclaim the truths of *YHVH El Shaddai*! Ask anyone, they will speak the truth regarding what I preach.' An official marched up to Jesus. He shouts, 'How dare you speak to the High Priest in that manner!' and strikes him across the face. 'Have I erred? If so, explain my action. But if I have spoken the truth, why do you strike me?' Annas fumes! He orders that the Nazarene be taken in chains to Caiaphas!

Midway in my following of proceedings, I came across a disciple in terrible distress. It was Peter! 'Peter, Peter, Can I help?' 'No one can help me now. I failed him, Manaen, denied that I ever knew him. If only I had that moment over again, I'm sure I'd have owned up to my link with Jesus! He warned me, Manaen. He said that Satan desires to sift me like wheat but that he would pray for me!' 'Then that is all you need,

Peter! What's more, you are better than the chaff which the wind tosses away! You are the golden wheat. Allow it to be planted in the ground. It will grow to be a great harvest. Peter, he will win the fight! The Sanhedrin must release him! Surely, they are "good enough" for that!'

I was never more aware of my privilege to be given access to the "holy halls of power". But where is Nicodemus? A lawyer informs me that he has not been summoned! Nicodemus most probably would not have entered the courts anyway: it was decreed that the Sanhedrin must not sit after sundown. The High Priest and his councillors were breaking the law!

The trial was a mockery! The Sanhedrin, with "you-know-who" sitting in the top chair, ranting on at this gentle, gracious man as though he were a murderer or near enough! Derogatory remarks were thrown at him. He was blindfolded. Then a scornful challenge came: 'prophesy, go on: who hit you?' Much similar abuse was hurled at him. How could I intervene? I saw no way!

As dawn was breaking, the Chief Priests and the teachers of The Law met together to discuss the situation. Jesus was brought before them. 'Tell us, are you the Messiah—Christ, "The Anointed One"? He answered, 'If I confess, you will not believe me and if I asked you that question, you would refuse to answer. From this time on, I will be seated at the right hand of *YHVH El Shaddai*—my Father in Heaven!' 'Are you declaring that you are the Son of God?' 'You are correct!' The inquisitors seized their chance! 'We need no further proof! We have no need of witnesses! He has condemned himself out of his own mouth!'

The whole assembly rose and tramped off to the Antonia Fortress in order to place the prisoner into the hands of Pontius Pilate—the current Roman Governor. Pilate's jurisdiction was administered from Caesarea but he was at present in Jerusalem to prevent any undue trouble emanating from the Passover Festival.

Pilate heard the complaint with a smirk! He could read the Jewish aristocracy better than they could themselves! 'What is the accusation?' 'Sir, this man proclaims a subversive doctrine. He refuses to pay the just taxes required by Rome. Of greater import is his claim to be a king—the Christ, in fact!' 'Is not this man from the Galilean region?' 'He is indeed, your honour!' Pilate's smirk broadened. 'This being the case, the Galilean comes under the jurisdiction of Herod Antipas! I cannot try the man!' Jesus would now be brought before my brother-in-law, Herod!

Herod Antipas was in his element! He had been yearning to finally face up to the Nazarene. Herod wanted to see a miracle! He threw question after question at Jesus but he received no answer! Jesus refused to comply with not so much as a retort from the onslaught!

Finally, Herod lived up—or should I say 'lived down' to the standard of his usual behaviour! He ordered that Jesus be dressed in an elegant, princely gown and, with this ignominious behaviour completed, the prisoner was sent off again to Pilate.

It was at that very moment that Jesus, obviously aware of my presence, turned and gazed on me with an expression of grace, of peace—yes, *shalom* peace. I knew then that he was the one in charge of the situation. But I also heard the bleak order that Jesus was to be returned to Pilate! It was on that infamous day that Herod Antipas and Pontius Pilate actually became friends. Cohorts in crime was my opinion of that liaison.

'I find no fault in this man!' Pilate declared. Not good enough, Pilate. Try again! Pilate summoned the Chief Priests. 'You gave me no basis for your claims! Herod could not point the finger of blame at him so sent him back to me. I tell you now, I find no fault in the man! He has done nothing deserving of the death penalty! I will punish him— though what for, I do not know—then, I will release him!'

'Pilate, it is your custom to release a prisoner during the Passover Festival. Away with this man; give us Barabbas in his place!' Though that man's name means 'son of the father', he is a convicted murderer!

The governor then questioned Jesus once more. 'Tell me, are you— as you say—the "King of the Jews"?' 'Is this your question or did others request that you ask this of me?' 'I am not a Jew. It was your people that handed you over to me. What did you really do?' 'It has been said that I am a king. You need to know that my Kingdom is not of this world!' 'You are a king, then!' 'Well said! It was for this reason I was born; it is the reason I came into this world: to testify to truth! People listen to truth!' 'What is truth?' The question remained unanswered but Pilate was staring TRUTH in the face and did not recognise it!

Pilate then presented himself to the Jewish leaders and the suddenly accumulated rabble to declare again, 'I find no fault in this man! Do you want me to release the "King of the Jews"?' 'No! Not him! give us Barabbas!' Standing among the crowd, I was nonplussed, horrified!

Pilate then ordered that Jesus be flogged, after which a hastily constructed crown was placed on his head—a crown of thorns that pierced the brow of this kingly man! Pilate too was living down to his reputation! Pilate announced his decision. 'You take him! You crucify him! As for me, I find no basis for a charge against him!' The custodians of Jewish Law then shouted, 'We have a law, the breaking of which demands the death penalty. The Nazarene claims to be the Son of God!' Pilate was plainly perplexed. He interrogated Jesus once more: 'Where do you come from?' Jesus now offered no reply. 'Do you refuse to answer me? Don't you realise that I have the power of life or death over you?' 'You would have no power over me unless it is granted by *YHVH El Shaddai*! Those who handed me over to you carry the greater sin!' That was enough for Pilate. The man should go free!

The reaction of the priests and the rabble to this verdict knew no bounds. They used their last throw of the dice! 'If you free this man, you are no friend of Caesar! The prisoner has declared himself to be a king! Therefore, he opposes Caesar!' Pilate knew, finally, that he had lost the argument! Jesus must die! Anyway, was it not expedient that one should die to placate the nation? 'Take him. Do what you will with him. I find no fault in him! I wash my hands of the matter!'

A spirit of festivity then broke out. The Jewish rulers had won the day! Jesus, the Nazarene, was to be crucified. Already suffering from the lashings given him, the prisoner was regaled into lifting a cross on which he would offer up his life. The procession to the location of his death was not to be a long one but, already, the prisoner was beginning to stagger under his burden. The Roman officer in charge of the "parade" could see the extremity of the prisoner's pain. He turned to a sturdy man standing by and ordered him to take charge of the cross. It seemed to me that the man did not mind the imposition. In fact, I'm sure he was keen to take the burden, help the prisoner in his pain!

No! No! My refuge! Not my grotto?! The host was headed there, to Golgotha—certainly, now, "the Place of the Skull". I could only stare at the grim spectacle. The soldiers, flaying the prisoner, driving him to make it to the summit, were obviously relieved at last to be on site. Three holes had been dug. Three? Two other men would be done to death on the crosses being prepared. The prisoners were thrust to the ground. Nails were hammered through the flesh of men agonising in excruciating pain. Finally, with a merciless thud, each cross (carrying its victim) was thrust into its hole made ready to receive the blood-stained wood. On the central cross a title was affixed: "The King of the Jews" in three languages. Meant to deride, the placard 'spoke' TRUTH. In spite of remonstrations, Pilate refused to modify the title. 'What I have written, I have written!' No one could argue with that proclamation.

The hours dragged on. What? What was that? An earthquake? In Jerusalem? Surely not! The sky is darkening. The city is losing light. It's only mid-afternoon. How strange. Strange, too, the utterings from the central cross. I hear the words, though faint, *Eloi, Eloi,* (My God), *why have You forsaken me?* Forsaken? Yeshua, forsaken? He continues: *I am poured out like water... My heart has melted...* But then: *They pierced my hands and feet... Praise God for He has not disdained the suffering of the afflicted one... All the ends of the Earth will remember and turn to the LORD... all will bow down before Him...* (Psalm 22).

Here is the Messiah: the *kebes*, Lamb of God, who takes the sin of the world upon himself though he has done no wrong. This is THE ATONEMENT DAY! *YHVH El Shaddai* is reconciling the world to Himself by means of *The Lamb, slain from the foundation of the world!*

One prisoner hurls abuse, the other cries, 'Please remember me when you come into your kingdom!' Jesus, also in extreme agony, replies, *You will be with me in Paradise today!*

He speaks again, *Father, forgive these people for they do not know what they are doing.* Never a truer word said nor prayed!

I thirst... What do they do? Send up a sponge soaked with vinegar? What kind of thirst can be cured with vinegar?

There's John. Standing with... Yes, it is the mother of Jesus! How can she bear the horror of this scene? In the depth of his agony, the son takes care of her! *John, please look after my Mother. Mother, receive John as your son!*

Suddenly there is a cry. I can describe it as no other than a declaration of triumph, of achievement! *It is finished!* All that his mission required is completed! Hallelujah! Yes! *"The Lamb of God"* has—through his utmost sacrifice—made it possible for humankind to escape their sinfulness! And I am one of them! At the time most likely for me to renounce my paltry level of faith in this man, my faith has firmed. I do believe that He was meant to take the sin of the world upon his shoulders and he succeeded for, here I stand now, a man of faith!

I hear then those unforgettable words: *Father I give my Soul, my Spirit, into Your hands.* Then, he had gone. He returned himself to Heaven!!! The Roman officer exclaimed, 'Truly, this man was a son of the gods.' I replied, 'Truly, he was the Son of God!'

As I descended that horror hill, Golgotha, I came upon Jeremiah's Grotto. Seeking consolation, I entered into my well-loved cavern and began to meditate on Jeremiah's triumph over tragedy. When all was lost, Jeremiah had been stirred by *YHVH's* immortal words:

*I have **loved** you, My people, with an everlasting love. With unfailing love, I have **drawn you** to Myself. I will **rebuild** you… He will **gather** His people as a shepherd does his flock for the LORD has **redeemed** Israel!* (Jeremiah 31, selected verses).

That is what has happened today! The LORD has laid upon Messiah the sins of the people. In him, the redemption price has been paid! We must tell the people—ALL the people—but, *HOW?*

A psalm was forming in my mind. I'd rely on my soul to hold it there.

THE SHADOW OF THE CROSS
(Choir: *Toplady*, 7.7.7.7.7.7.)

Darkness shadowed all the earth
When our Lord was crucified;
Day became the darkest night,
Nature sorrowed in the gloom.
Sun and moon retired to grieve,
Veiled from the Eternal Light.

Death had entered in this scene,
Strident in its violent might;
Purity was slaughtered here,
Righteousness was overthrown.
By Satanic powers unleashed,
Gone from us our Saviour dear.

He was taken to a cross,
Raised upon its rugged frame.
Who selected such a death,
For a man so innocent?
Who willed Jesus Christ to die?
Who? The LORD of Heaven and Earth!

God sent not His only Son
To the world, there to condemn
Every soul through all Earth's days;
His great gift would save the world!
Calvary was meant for me,
But–in grace–Christ took my place!

When he cried, 'Abba, it's done!',
Jesus knew accomplishment!
Satan would not claim this day;
Less than victor, death was done–
Never would it conqueror be,
Never dim God's radiant day!

I went to find Nicodemus. His despair was heart-wrenching. 'Manaen, I must go to my friend Joseph—you know, the rich man from Arimathea, he is a secret disciple of Jesus as am I. We must make plans to bury Jesus without delay—before sundown. Help me please.'

Joseph was pleased to offer his recently purchased burial plot that was situated quite near to Golgotha. We pleaded our cause before Pilate who was obviously relieved to rid himself of the whole unsettling task. When we returned to Golgotha, the body of Jesus had been taken down from the cross. He had died prematurely according to the soldiers. 'We used a spear, of course, to check the status of the body. Strangely, both blood and water flowed from the wound. It would appear that this man actually died of a broken heart!' Why am I not surprised?

What did surprise me was that the tomb of Joseph was located just across the way within a garden, a well-loved garden—the garden of Manaen and Maryam! Because I was the youngest (and sturdiest) of the three, I elected to carry the lifeless body. Nicodemus had brought with him a mixture of aloes and myrrh. He and Joseph wrapped the body in linen as is our custom. The tomb—a sepulchre—was sealed before the setting of the sun. All was done in accordance with The Law for it was the "Day of Preparation". After sunset, it would be the *sabbath*. Then no further work could be attempted. We noted that Pilate had set a guard to ensure that no one tampered with the sepulchre.

Exhausted, greatly in need of the comforting arms of my beloved, I went home. Maryam was beside herself with worry. What had become of me? Would she see me again after the tragic events of this day? I assured her that Nicodemus, Joseph and I had fulfilled everything necessary to secure the body and that the sepulchre was now under guard. But life for us would never be the same again. Mine was now what could only be called, a "post-death" allegiance to "*the Lamb of God*"! But I despaired for what might have been.

It was the morning after *sabbath*, the first day of the week. I awoke before dawn, roused Maryam and asked her to accompany me to our garden. I was in need of *shalom* peace. Perhaps I could regain it there. As we approached, I was amazed to find an open tomb!

16. A DISPLACED STONE

'What a beautiful dawn Maryam! There's a veritable glow in the garden!' We had exited the city via the Damascus Gate and were crossing now over into our precious haven. There was a well-worn pathway into the heart of the garden and we made our way through the almond blossoms so evocative of past promises which have held true through all the years of our marriage. We are deeply happy in this garden.

Our first view of the burial site, however, had filled us with apprehension. Grave robbers? Sanhedrin machinations? We could only surmise. We became aware that we were no longer alone. Another stood by our side. 'What is troubling you in this wonderful dawn?' 'Our friend, the Nazarene—Jesus—was laid to rest in this sepulchre but it has been opened! Where are the soldiers? How could this have happened?'

'Why are you searching for the dead when you are standing with the living, my friends?' That voice! I'd have known it anywhere! *Kebes*! 'Jesus! It is you! It can't be you! It is you! It can't be true. Yet, here you are… Are you… a ghost?' 'My friends, ghosts have no earthly form. Look at me. Here are my hands. See the wounds. Healed now. Forever, healed! Look at my hands. Know the truth. I have risen. I am alive, eternally alive!'

We stood with him then, sharing things that must be said. While we had not lost our faith in him, we had held no hope that the Messiah could fulfil all that the Scriptures had foretold of him. The Golgotha horror had taken every hope. I did explain, however, that it was while standing at his cross, I had come to a living faith which would not be shaken. 'And, Lord—let me call you "Lord" for such you are—where are the soldiers now?' He replied, 'There will be an inane story put about: "His disciples stole the body, don't you know". It will be believed, except by those who come to faith because I am alive eternally.

'Manaen, Maryam, I know of your faith. Your future is secure. There will be sorrow, yes. But know this truth, I will stand with you until the very end! You will speak for me and live for me and you will find new strength to fulfil the role in store for you. And I will be with you! You will understand just what I mean before too many days are done. Now, please, go to Nicodemus. Give to him the news!'

We felt that our hearts were embraced before we departed with this unprecedented news:

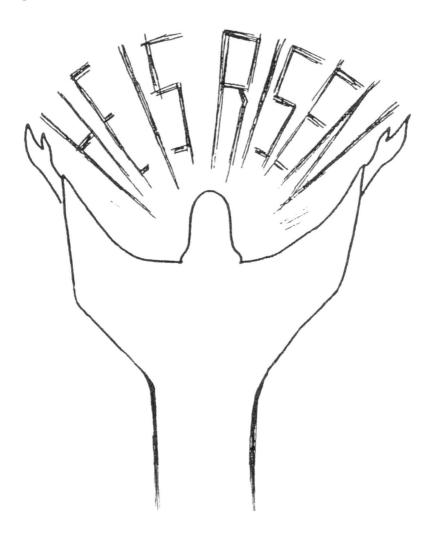

As we hurried through the garden, it was with a deep joy that we saw Peter and John rushing to the empty tomb. Obviously, they had already heard the news!

Have you ever been the bearer of Good News! Gospel News? What of the best news ever? 'JEUS IS ALIVE!' That's the news Maryam and I carried to Nicodemus! Unforgettable, his response. Unbelievable... Incredible... Want-to-believable... Astound-able... Acceptable... Rejoice-able! We read it all on his dearly loved features! 'Really? Manaen, how can it be? And yet I see the truth of it written all over you! I must go to Joseph! We will come to you later in the day.'

What an hour it had been. Never-to-be-forgotten. Yet we managed breakfast. I think that we were both suffering from a mixture of shock, surprise, elation, joy and deep soul satisfaction. We savoured that and, though we didn't chatter on, we found contentment now. We did wonder what David would make of the news when he returned home. Oh, how we hoped he would rejoice! Maryam took charge of the dishes and I went to fetch my writing kit. A new psalm was stirring in my soul:

CHRIST IS RISEN
(Choir: *Austria* 8.7.8.7. D. Trochaic)

Rise the sun in radiant splendour,
Clothe the sky in peerless blue,
Dress the world in shining garments,
Celebrate a dawn that's new!
Never has there been rejoicing
Such as this that greets the dawn;
Christ is risen: Hallelujah!
All the world has been reborn.

Claim the dawn! its light resplendent
Greets the valley of despair
Where a garden, lovely garden,
Waits its glorious news to share.

Rock is rending, burst asunder,
Death cannot its Victim hold.
Christ is risen! Hallelujah!
All the world sees joy unfold.

Morning breaks on visions splendid,
Glowing colours paint the earth;
A new day has dawned upon us
Day of grace, the day for faith!
Hope has come that knows no ending,
Knowledge of Eternity.
Christ is risen: Hallelujah!
All the world may now go free.

How does one return to some sense of normal life after such life-changing events? Of necessity I came once more to the Temple Courts and on into the Hall of Hewn Stones to find Nicodemus awaiting my arrival. His was more than a happy smile! 'Come with me,' he invited. 'You shouldn't miss this!' Together, we made our way into the Sanhedrin. Questions were being slung about. Excuses offered, none accepted. Caiaphas slouched in his seat, a querulous frown upon his face! 'What happened at that sepulchre?' 'Where is the body?' 'What does Herod say?' 'Why hasn't Pilate taken charge of things?' 'What of those rumours that the Nazarene would rise from the dead after three days?'

'Enough! I've heard enough!' Caiaphas screamed! He had now taken charge of things, explained the situation—not that the actuals would be reported in these hallowed halls! Nicodemus had it on good authority that the soldiers had been given a large sum of money to "keep their counsel" (on pain of death)! They were to spread a story that the disciples had come to take the body away while they slept. Nicodemus turned to me with barely concealed humour at my comment, 'But, how would they have known who stole the body, as they say, if they were all asleep?' 'Precisely, my friend. Precisely! Come, let us go from here!'

David had returned by the time I arrived home. He was aware that things were astir in the city. Strange stories were whispered behind the hand of covert commentators! *'Abba*, the weirdest rumours are hanging about the city streets! People are suggesting that the Nazarene is no longer dead! How on Earth can anyone come up with such a dullard donkey view as that?!' 'No one could make up a story like that, son, except when it is true!' 'What are you saying? Surely you don't... You do! How can you say such a thing?' 'Son, your mother and I have spoken with him today! This morning. In our special garden. You know the place.' *'Abba*, I don't know why you are telling me this. You haven't lost your reasoning powers. No! No! Where's *emi*? Let me see what she has to say about what you thought you saw. *Emi*, come and put us right!' 'My son, I've heard. My dear boy, I nod my head. It's true!'

'Mother, Father, you were dazzled by the morning light. You saw what you wanted to see! Dead men don't walk. Dead men don't talk!' 'Never-the-less, my son, it's true!' *'Emi, Abbi*, I know you would not lie to me. You think you know you saw... But, as for me, unless I see him for myself, I will not, I cannot believe the Nazarene is alive!' 'David, please: do not be grieved. Don't go!' But David had left. The door had slammed! I turned to Maryam. 'The day will come when he will see, for himself, that what we say, what we've seen, is true.' The day had begun so wonderfully but evening has brought a gloom no sinking sun could bequeath. On balance, though, we knew our joys, we knew our hopes!

The Passover was now well past. Life settled back into some sense of normality. I met Simon (the disciple also known as Peter) and the two sons of Zebedee—James and John—one day. By now they were aware that Maryam and I had met with Jesus so Peter explained that they were departing for the Galilee region. Their Rabbi was to meet with them there. They knew now that they still had much to learn. (Not as much as I do, I thought as they hurried on).

Within the month, they had returned. In seeking some news of Jesus from the men, I was informed that he was soon to depart. 'Don't be concerned, Manaen. He said that he would not leave us as orphans! He said that he would come to us.' Can't think what he meant by that: he would leave them but he'd be with them. The thing is, he knows what he meant and we will discover the truth of it without undue delay!

There was a mist on the Mount of Olives. Unusual for the time of year. Then I saw the eleven disciples—friends—of Jesus hurrying up the slopes. It seemed a good idea to investigate (rather than front up to the Temple requirements of the day). I crossed the *Kidron* and hurried up the slopes of Olivet. And there he was. I'm glad I had trekked up that mighty hill! I saw him and he saw me! I still thought of him as my *Kebes* but, now, he was also the *Mashiach*, Messiah—Christ! *Yeshua*, Jesus: Saviour of the world. He smiled at me! He raised his hand. I realised that it was a "farewell" wave! He was leaving us. What was it that his men had said? He would depart but he would come to them? Away? But not away? There was something more I had to learn!

But Jesus had gone. Suddenly, the mist had surrounded him. A mist, a cloud, does not "lift" a man; but when the mist had gone, Jesus had also gone! I realised that he couldn't be floating up in the sky! But he was gone. He had returned to his Father in Heaven. Jesus was "lifted" into the Eternal Dimension. I have long thought that Heaven is further away than a galaxy but also—at the same time—nearer than breathing. Could it be that Jesus is now nearer than breathing? I would go to my writing kit. I had something to say! It was time for a new psalm to be sung.

THE FINGERPRINTS OF GOD

(Choir: *There's mercy still for thee* D.C.M.)

I found the fingerprints of God
Upon the radiant dawn;
In forest glens, on mountain heights,
His wondrous works are shown.
A tender leaf, a wayside flower,
His rainbow on the cloud,
The sparkling joy in children's eyes
Reveal the touch of God.

The Word of God once moved
Upon Creation's Day;
He brought all living things to birth;
Lord, move in me, I pray.

I found the signature of God
Upon the sacred page;
The story of the King of kings
Speaks truth for every age.
Redeeming love at Calvary, *
Outpoured in matchless grace,
Is written large across His word;
He signs the way to peace.

The Lord of Life has breathed,
Inspiring hope today;
Imprinting Gospel truths in me;
Lord, breathe in me, I pray.

I found the footprints of my Lord
Upon the human road;
He bids me tread on holy ground

For He would ease my load.
In conversations of the soul,
His sacred voice I hear!
I know His tread along my road,
I now discern Him near.

O Lord of Love, now come,
Companion me today;
You bring abundant grace to me;
Lord, walk with me, I pray.

* Calvary: Hebrew, Golgotha

17. THE WIND STORM

'Manaen, we have that large reception room that is now hardly used. We could invite the Nazarene's friends to share with us in fellowship. What do you think?' 'Beloved! What a marvellous idea. I'll go to Simon Peter—I never know what to call the man; I think it's "Peter" now. Yes, Peter it will be: he's as solid as a rock anyway! He seems to be taking charge of all that's going on. He can spread the word. This room can become a sacred place. We'll have no need to stand outside the Temple's Holy Place and expect the priests to pray for us! We all can become priests. We all can speak to *YHVH El Shaddai* on behalf of the needy people in this city and beyond. I'll go to him right now.'

Hardly a day had passed before our home was crammed with people—happy, joyful people. Men and women; no discrimination in this throng of worshippers, for that is what we did: we worshipped God. We thanked him for his grace, for the revelation he has made in Jesus, the Christ, for the miracle of the resurrection, for this new deep peace pervading us, for the sense of expectation that was upon us.

Peter explained that it would not be long before the disciples of Jesus would receive a mandate from Heaven to become apostles—they had been "students" (disciples) of the Lord; soon they would become His "ambassadors"!

My work at the Temple was largely curtailed because Nicodemus would be, most often, found at our home! Matters of Law were attended as needs required but we were happy just to be rejoicing together with the large numbers who would come each day. Among the many were Mary, the Mother of Jesus and also his family. Wonderful! His brothers now were fully engaged with the group. I understand that Jesus had, as he had done with Maryam and me, appeared to James—his brother— on the morning of his resurrection. That reunion would have been enough for James to accept his brother as his Lord!

During the days before Pentecost—so called because this feast occurred fifty days following the Sabbath of Passover—another man was chosen to replace Judas, the betrayer. Matthias was selected. There we were praying for something to happen. And it did! It was the dawn of Pentecost!

Suddenly, a mighty wind stirred up among us. How come? The doors and windows were closed. This wind now caught us up in an ecstasy! It was the *ruach* "Wind"—the very Breath of God! Here, present with us, the very Spirit of the Lord! Filling us! Empowering us! What looked like split tongues, resembling flames of fire came down upon us. We began to shout in words we had never learned!

'Manaen, I know what you said! I've never spoken in the *lingua franca*, never learned Greek. How did I understand what you said?' 'What did I say, my beloved?' 'You said: *"Thus says the LORD: I will pour out My Spirit upon all people!"*' 'Yes! And you are right! I spoke not in Hebrew but in Greek! The words came from the prophet Joel. Today that prophecy is fulfilled! But look, Maryam, look! Everyone is rushing out into the street for crowds are flocking to see what has been making that noise like a gale force wind when everything is so calm outside! There's pandemonium all about! Questions asked. Answers given. Ah! Peter is taking charge.'

'My name is Simon, also known as Peter, Apostle of the Risen Messiah! I know you are all wondering what has been happening. You're so wrong to think that we have all drunk far too much wine! Too early for that, my friends—even if we were so inclined! Let me explain. You will need to listen carefully to what I say. You who are visitors to Jerusalem: you have heard these men and women suddenly speaking in your native tongues. Not possible? Well, No! We have never spoken in different languages before. You have a right to ask, to know what is going on here!

'I here proclaim to you all that you are witnessing the fulfilment of the prophecy of Joel who recorded the words of *YHVH El Shaddai*:

In the last days I will pour out My Holy Spirit upon all people… Young men will see visions and old men will dream dreams. I will pour out My Spirit upon both men and women and they will proclaim Good News. You will witness wonders—signs—before the coming of the great and glorious day of the LORD! Everyone who calls upon the name of the LORD will be saved!' (Joel 2:28-32).

'Now, let me tell you about Jesus! Wicked men put him to death. But God raised him from the dead. It was impossible for death to hold him! King David testified of him:

My heart is glad... for you will not abandon me to the grave nor will you allow your Holy One to decay. You have made known to me the path of life; you will fill me with joy in your presence. (Psalm 16:8-11).

'I tell you now: David did die and his tomb is still here—in Jerusalem! But David was a prophet. He knew he had been promised by *YHVH El Shaddai* that one of his descendants would sit on the Everlasting Throne. God has raised David's descendant, Jesus, to Life! We are witnesses to this truth! Therefore, let all Israel be assured of this: God has made Jesus, whom you crucified, both Lord and Christ!'

'What can we do? What can we do to receive the salvation that is given through the risen Christ?' 'Be sorry for your sins. Be made clean in your soul! Be filled with his Spirit of Power. The promised Holy Spirit—the Spirit of the Living Christ—has come upon us now and He is able to make us what we were meant to be!'

What a wonderful, never-to-be-forgotten day! By the end of it, over three thousand people opened up their sinned-stained lives to be forgiven, cleansed, and enabled to live in a new way, empowered by the Holy Spirit "Wind": the *ruach—pnuema*!

I know my boy! He is a man now, of course. The declarations of Peter concerning King David have caused me once more to mourn for my boy! Maryam and I miss his boisterous presence in our home. Yes, we mourn for him. I understood more fully the grief of King David mourning his son Absalom. Our David is no Absalom! Our David is a good man! His zeal is for the Law. For Jerusalem. For *YHVH*! Yes, there is a goodness in our son.

I saw him just yesterday. He waved at me. I caught the message in that wave. He holds no grudge that his Mother and I should avow our trust in One he thinks in mouldering in the grave! But he will have no part of it. His day would come. We longed to see him in our home once more. If only he could meet a woman whom he could love. We were sure it would mellow him! David, do come home to us! David's aims and purposes, however, were firmly set in the Zealot project to overthrow Rome. They could not bide their time to await a better day for Rome's demise. They knew not that day would only come in God's good time!

Nicodemus had quite a story to tell upon my return to his office at the Temple. 'Do you remember that poor crippled man who would rattle his cup each day at the Gate Beautiful in the hope of a handout to keep him in food and lodging? He's been a fixture there for years! But he's not rattling his cup today, Manaen! He's not there!' 'Where is he?' 'In the Temple Court, leaping and shouting and praising *YHVH*! Manaen, he's been cured!' 'Cured?' 'Oh, it is wonderful! Splendiferous! I'm told that Peter and John walked by. The cup was rattled! Peter spoke up, 'I'm sorry that we have no coins for you. But what we do have we will give to you! In the name of Jesus of Nazareth, stand up! You will be able to walk. You will be healed!'

'The man stood up. Felt his legs. Took a step. Began to walk! He's been here, in the Temple grounds ever since, leaping about and praising God. He can walk! Manaen, the thing is: words have been spoken about it in the Sanhedrin. The Sadducees in particular are incensed! They prattle on. 'The man's been a malingerer all his life.' 'He pleads his cause at the Gate so that he's had no need to work.' 'And now he's making an ungodly spectacle of himself!' 'Something's got to be done about these never-ending rumours about a resurrected Christ!'

There were indeed some "thunder-claps" in the near vicinity! Matters were being mulled about and Nicodemus—and his right-hand man (me)—were given responsibility for conjuring up a suitable means of returning things to a sedate state of affairs!

I must admit that our plan was quite splendid! Call Peter and John before the Sanhedrin. Let them testify as to their message and their methods. We knew, of course, that they were living and moving in the power of the Holy Spirit. They would not be tongue-tied! Also, it was a powerful means whereby the Sanhedrin would hear the truth of all that was happening. Some might even accept the truth of the *Gospel*—Good News—message and find themselves transformed. Surprise, surprise! The plan was agreed!

A cohort of priests, Sadducees and the captain of the Temple guard approached Peter and John while they were in the middle of their daily testimonial to the risen Saviour. Both men were seized but, because it was already evening, it was necessary to place them in prison for fear they might abscond! In the meantime, many who had heard Peter and John's message were convinced. They chose to also become followers of Jesus. The number of those converted to "the Jesus Way" was now about five thousand!

Next morning there was a full house! Annas was there, as was Caiaphas—who would be High priest today? I wondered grimly. In fact, their whole family was there, in the hope of seeing quite a spectacle, no doubt. The questions commenced: 'By what power or authority do you flaunt yourselves in such an unruly manner?' Peter took the floor!

Nicodemus and I were at once assured that our strategy had worked! We were well aware that the Sanhedrin were also investigating, testing our worth as their "envoys". Peter, obviously filled with the Holy Spirit, spoke with confidence and passion yet was quite circumspect. We were so proud of him! His explanation flowed as the truth was exposed!

'If we are being called to account because of an act of kindness shown to a crippled man in much need of healing, then know this: it is in the Name of Jesus, the *Mashiach* (Messiah), whom you crucified but whom God raised from death, that this man—I call him now to stand before you as testimony to God's work in his life—is healed. Behold the man, he's over forty years of age! Now hear this: Jesus, *the Stone you builders rejected, is the One who has become the Cornerstone!* Salvation is to be found in no other than He! There is no other name given under Heaven by which we must be saved!'

The Sanhedrin was astounded! This "unlettered" fisherman from the despised northern climes had stood his ground, left them speechless! The Council as a whole took stock of these two men and noted that they had been with Jesus! They also concluded that the man had been healed. It was proof enough. After a secluded conference, it was determined that Peter and John should go free. When the verdict was handed down, however, both were admonished and then directed to no longer go about preaching such an unorthodox message.

Peter could do no other than to exclaim: 'Be your own judge. Is it right to obey God or the dictates of men, be they judge and jury? We cannot but speak of the things that we have both heard and seen!'

Both men were instructed—on pain of punishment—not to speak of the Nazarene again! Peter and John were now "marked men" but nothing could restrain them. The God-given message of salvation was delivered in the power of the Holy Spirit. It was *Gospel* News: Good News, news now in the hands of men transformed to preach without constraint!

It was not long before Peter and a number of the brethren were taken into custody for transgressing the edict of the Sanhedrin! Neither Nicodemus nor I could save him now. Only God could intervene! The Community of Faith—as we were prone to call ourselves—came together to pray for the men whose lives, we assumed, were now held by a precarious, fraying thread! When the situation seemed beyond redemption, who should stand to his feet but Gamaliel—a Pharisee and leading teacher of The Law! Here was a revered leader prepared to say a word on behalf of the men. He ordered the prisoners to be taken from the Sanhedrin and then he began to speak:

'Men of Israel. Consider very carefully what you are about to do.' He then proceeded to outline some unfortunate past happenings. In bringing his argument to a conclusion, Gamaliel then advised, 'With regard to this present case before the court, my advice is to leave them be! If what they are saying and doing is of their own devising, they are sure to fail! If, on the other hand, this phenomenon is of *YHVH El Shaddai*, you will not be able to quench their powerful proclamations! You will find, instead, that you are fighting against God!'

I don't think that I had ever seen the Sanhedrin swayed from their determination so quickly and profoundly. The prisoners were, however, flogged before their chains were unbolted and the captives freed. Peter and his friends went out into the public arena rejoicing because they had been counted worthy to suffer the disgrace of imprisonment for the cause of Christ!

18. BREAKING DOWN BARRIERS

As is the way of it, when large but disparate groups endeavour to merge as one, some disputes surfaced to the effect that Grecian Jews began to feel a discrimination at the hands of the Hebraic Jews. Widows were not being attended as they ought. Children were being left without due care. A conference was called. The apostles determined that they should not be diverted from their major ministry—that of prayer and the proclamation of the Gospel! Something, however, must be done to quell the disquiet.

When the decision of the apostles was reported to me by Nicodemus, I marvelled at the wisdom of selecting seven men who would take control of all the social needs of the Community. What blessed my soul was the requirement that these men were to be filled with the Holy Spirit and wisdom! Who but the apostles would have thought that people whose serving hands only were required, would need to have a strong spiritual base for all their activities! I rejoiced in that!

Of particular interest to the entire Community of Faith was that the men selected for this special ministry had included Nicolas, a proselyte—a man from Antioch who was a convert to Judaism! Amazing things were happening. The Community continued to grow in numbers and in strength. What is more, there were now a number of priests who had become obedient to the claims of Christ! They were now integral to the membership of the Community of Faith.

One of the "Serving Seven", a man by the name of Stephen, was an outstanding man of faith and action! Jews of the Diaspora began to argue with him but they found their antagonism was of no avail. Stephen was more than a match for them. Such a situation could not be abided and some scurrilous reports were made to the powers that be. 'This man Stephen is putting about blasphemous words against Moses and against *YHVH El Shaddai*!'

The populace was stirred and the resultant unrest caused the Elders and teachers of The Law to act. Stephen was brought before the Sanhedrin. There was a full House, including Nicodemus and myself. We were, therefore, able to gather that the accusations and the responses made were exacerbating an already extremely serious situation. Could Stephen stand his ground among this milling multitude of malevolence?

The speech of Stephen before his accusers deserved go down in the annals of the most superb addresses to be delivered in the Sanhedrin. This man, so new to the Community of Faith, knew The Law and the history of our people, the interventions of *YHVH El Shaddai* in the affairs of humankind. 'From Abraham to the Righteous One, God's own people have persecuted, have murdered God's prophets! Compounding all, you have killed the Righteous One. You received The Law but you have failed to obey it.'

That was the statement deemed above all else to be that which signed Stephen's death warrant. I deeply grieve the need to place on record what happened next. Here I am, a man steeped in The Law from my early years at the Rabbinic School in Bethlehem, through to the hallowed halls of the Temple's Rabbinic School and tutored by such men as Nicodemus. I must listen to the condemnation to death of a man most innocent! Lies, hatred, jealousy, bigotry had won the day.

'Look, look,' Stephen cried. 'I see the glory of God and there he stands: Jesus—at the right hand of *YHVH El Shaddai*! Look! Look! Heaven has opened to us here!' I do not doubt the vision of the condemned man!

The members of the Sanhedrin, almost to a man, blocked their ears. They rushed at him, yelling, 'Stone him! Stone him!' Stephen was dragged from the Sanhedrin, out beyond the city gates where his murderous executioners began their deadly work. How horrified I was to see Saul, the "Terror from Tarsus", standing by the executioners, minding all their cloaks. There was a smile of acquiescence upon his Pharisaic face! Would there be a hope for Saul in Heaven? I doubted it!

The day of Stephen's martyrdom marked the commencement of a great persecution breaking out which caused the scattering of most members of the Community of The Faith. Stephen's body was taken and buried with due reverence by faithful people intent on recognising his works of grace and proclamations of power among all the people. The apostles remained in the city to assure their work would continue. Those, however, who had departed for safer climes, took their faith and its message with them! The Good News went wherever they went!

Philip was particularly mobile. His itinerary—north to Samaria, south to Gaza— revealed him to be a man more intent on sharing his faith than escaping from his adversaries. When news of the remarkable response of people to Philip's ministry reached them, the brethren in Jerusalem asked Peter and John to investigate the Samaritan reports. With their coming, there was a great outpouring of the Holy Spirit. Peter then went west to Lydda and on to Joppa.

It was a period of great rejoicing. Philip was instrumental in leading an Ethiopian proselyte to faith in Christ. As the man was returning to his homeland in Africa, this would mark the movement of the *Gospel* beyond Israel!

Peter's ministry did not conclude at Joppa. In fact, it marked another turning point in the sharing of The Word! Yes! Philip had introduced a man already engaged in a study of the Hebrew Scriptures—a proselyte to the Hebrew faith—to Jesus, the One to whom those very Scriptures pointed. And now Peter, against his personal inclination actually, was to take the Good News to the Gentile world!

I delighted in the news he brought to the Community of Faith upon his return to Jerusalem. It was an astounding account of how the Lord was able to break through into his rather parochial outlook on how a Jew should behave when confronted with the behaviour patterns of non-Jews! He actually shared a prayer conversation! 'What me? Eat "unclean" food, Lord? Never! You know I would never allow my principles to be pushed aside!' That's what Peter told us. He also explained that the Lord had admonished him. 'Peter, please, do not consider as impure that which I have made clean!'

Well, Peter saw the Light! He had gone with some messengers to Caesarea where he was to meet the Roman Centurion, a man by the name of Cornelius. Peter discovered him to be a righteous man who listened eagerly to the apostle and was led to faith in Christ! Peter's news delighted the Community of Faith though some were rather slow to rejoice! 'Is it right that Gentiles be given access into the Kingdom of God?' Some people are so slow to learn!

Peter explained his vision. He had seen a sheet floating down towards him from over the Mediterranean Sea. The sheet had been filled with many, what we would call, unclean animals. He had heard the Lord's voice, 'Arise, Peter, kill and eat!' The vision was repeated three times before Peter "got the message": 'Peter, I can make the "unclean" *CLEAN*!' Peter was being instructed to share his faith beyond the borders of Israel—its geography and its mind!

Peter's testimony concerning his own slowness to obey the clear instructions of the Lord and the remarkable results of his final decision to go to Caesarea found no further objections! The Community as a whole accepted this new directive, rejoicing in the Lord with comments such as 'Praise God! He has granted even the Gentiles their right to faith in Jesus, the Christ!'

David came home! My own *em* and *abbi* taught me the value of home—it is more than the *bayith*, house, it is where the heart is at rest, serene, content. It is where I feel most safe and secure! As I entered the room to find David with his *em*, my beloved Maryam, in close and happy conversation, I saw again the value of a haven where minds and hearts may mingle in the harmony that "family" allows.

David looked up. There was pleasure written on his face as he greeted me. What a joy for me. 'You're home! It is so good to see you, David. How are you? Oh, it is a joy… Tell me…' Maryam had to curb my enthusiasm and did so with some well-placed comments of her own! I began to listen then. David had his questions too.

'*Abba*, I've been looking at the recent happenings in Jerusalem. There is a different atmosphere in the city. I can't put my finger on it. I'm of the mind that it seems to stem from that crippled man who no longer sits at the Gate Beautiful begging for handouts! Where is he now? Is it right? Is he cured? If so, I'd really like to know just how it was done! There are all sorts of stories floating about. Some people are even suggesting that it was the work of the Nazarene.

'No, Father, hear me out! I can't fling things that I can't believe, or don't understand, under the carpet forever. There is a logical answer. If I could believe the rumours, I would be the first to stand up for him. I can't *Abba*, I can't see the logic of a dead man walking, talking and changing all the whys and wherefores of our lives! My chosen lifestyle suits me just fine. My mind is well grounded in the faith of our fathers and my soul is imbedded in The Law. Why should I look for a new way to live my life?'

In taking the time now to look at and to listen to my son, I allowed myself to observe a number of things which enabled me to "read" this young man at greater depth than in recent times. My deep concern for his well-being had clouded the major issues that were fermenting in his mind.

To a large extent, here was the crux of the problem. In his heart, David had never left home! His is a deep and abiding love for his parents—for our nurturing, our loving and tender care for his life and learning. We had never deviated from the love we felt for him. In the soul of us, we are as one. It was the matter of the mind that exposed the disparate nature of our attitudes and reactions to the many challenges and obstacles which presented themselves with an unsettling regularity! Yes! This is exactly it! What is the difference between a challenge and an obstacle? It will depend on how we think of it and whether we face it or run from it.

The realisation came that I could not change David's mind for him. I could pray for him, advise him, but I needed to give him space to deal with the obstacles and face the challenges that would surely come to him. In the meantime, we shared our news, gave some explanations for our point of view. Speaking from experience, we sought to give reason for the changes that our son saw in us.

Yes! The Nazarene had made a difference in our lives. I think David saw the truth of this—it, surely, is so evident. The matter of our faith was more difficult to open for discussion. 'What are the differences between faith, fiction, and fact, David?' It was so good to see the boy— sorry, the young man—chewing over that. Give him his due, the question was not treated with distain.

At the end of the day, I realised that David needed more time to respond adequately to all we had shared on that very special evening. He remained with us. That was our unbounded joy. What raised our hopes for him was that, on this night, there was no departure with the slamming of a door. He was content to be with us! In the heart of me, I felt that David was beginning to cast aside some obstacles so that the challenges could present themselves. I was well aware that my son did not lack courage—one couldn't bind himself to the mind-set of the Zealots if lacking in courage. His courage may yet win the battle for him. His soul would find its true home when his mind accepted The Truth.

What David had yet to face was the challenge to align his courage with that of faith! David had yet to learn that faith does not come with sight. Faith is born in the moment when a person realises a truth and is prepared to accept it even though the proof of it has yet to be visualised! Insight is always to be preferred over eyesight. Eyesight will bring the proof *after* the realisation, the recognition, of Truth! I understand that Jesus once said, *I AM the Truth… The Truth shall make you free. When the truth makes you free, you shall be free indeed!*

I felt a new psalm welling up from within and realised that it should be recorded. Perhaps David may read it one day and be glad!

LIGHT IS SHINING
(Choir: *Hold the Fort* 8.5.8.5. Chorus: 'Prayer')

Light is shining, ever shining
On the sacred page,
Bearing Truth's illumination,
Answers for our age.

Light is gleaming, always gleaming,
Over land and sea,
Bringing courage for our weakness
As we make our plea.

Light is beaming, brightly beaming,
Filling us with hope,
Faith for doubting, sight for blindness,
Life of endless scope.

Light is streaming, constant streaming
From the Lord of Life;
Light enough to guide our pathway
And to ease our grief.

Light is claiming, rightly claiming
Through the Living Word,
We may turn to Light from darkness
By the grace of God!

Prayer
Shine Your Light upon our sadness,
Turn our night to day;
Light that shimmers on our gladness,
Let us shine we pray.

19. A RIOT WITH ROCKS

King Herod Agrippa was now flexing his royal muscles! He proceeded to have a number of the faithful imprisoned, intending to bring as much harm as possible to our friends! James, the brother of John, was cut down mercilessly by a sword. When Herod saw how much James' death pleased the Jewish leaders, he intensified his evil edicts. An onslaught of unprecedented persecution broke out in Jerusalem.

Peter found himself in the midst of the unmitigated struggles to keep ahead of the relentless badgering and belligerence. Again, he saw the prison cells—from the inside! The Community of The Faith came together in the home of Mary, the mother of young John Mark, to pray for Peter's release. He had been kept in prison over the Passover for his eventual trial. There was Peter, awaiting "the inevitable", chained between two soldiers with sentries on guard at the entrance to his cell. Those men were certainly making sure that they would not lose their man before the trial!

Peter was soundly asleep. Suddenly, he was awakened by a sharp prod as a bright light revealed an angel—a messenger from Heaven—standing by him. 'Quick! Get up!' The chains on Peter's wrists fell to the ground. 'Put on your cloak and your sandals and follow me!' They walked together out from the prison. Peter told us later that he thought he was dreaming! This was not really happening to him! Past the first group of guards. Then, the second. This must be a dream! Still here he was, on the outside of the prison and its bars! When the iron gates yielded, Peter knew he was free. Then, the angel left him.

We were, at the same time, at prayer for Peter. Where was our faith? One of our company—a young woman named Rhoda—answered a knock at the door. It was Peter! Rhoda rushed in to give us the news! 'Rhoda, don't be crazy! Use your brains! It can't be Peter. He's in prison! Perhaps it's his angel.' 'But I'm sure…' 'Sit down, Rhoda, come and pray with us for his release.' We went to prayer again. The knocking continued. Another went to the door. Oh yes! It was Peter! No doubt of it. I say again, where was our faith—mine included?!

Herod's anger knew no bounds. When Peter could not be found, the guards were executed. Jerusalem could never be the same after this atrocity! Rocks were hurled, swords were swung, assassinations carried out. One day, my David stood close by an altercation between the sword swingers and the stone throwers when a wayward stone hit my son, my only son! Blood gushed from his head. A zealot friend hurried to the Temple where I was engaged in matters pertaining to The Law. I rushed to him. I saw there was no hope of recovery. David's life was ebbing fast.

'My son, my son! I'd have taken that rock for you! Please stay… Don't leave…' 'Someone, go for Maryam. Go! Go! Please tell her to come.' Maryam arrived just before the end. 'My boy, how I long to stanch this blood…' '*Abba… Em…* I love you… Everything is all right now! I see Him coming near to me… I know it… is… the… Nazarene… He is my Lord! I've found my faith, my… Life… *Abbi, Emi*, Goodbye… Yes, Lord, I am r e a d y…' With our son's testimony of faith, he was gone. I knew, within the heart of me, that he was escorted into Heaven by my *kebes*—Lamb, who will, one day, heal this sin-sick world. David was buried with sorrow mingled with joy!

'Maryam, my love, we must leave Jerusalem. Herod Agrippa will not abide a princess being associated with the Nazarene. He means to annihilate us all! I will go to Nicodemus, take my leave of him. Please pack the things with which you cannot part. Don't forget my writing kit.' I went to an appointed place. It was no longer safe for me, or for Nicodemus, to be seen at the Sanhedrin. I would be so sorry to leave this city of my heritage. Perhaps, I would never gaze upon its Temple, its towers, its walls, again. But stone-work (no matter how grandiose) cannot build a city. A city is its people and I must now part from them.

'Dear Nicodemus, will you come with us?' 'My friend of years, my place is here. My voice must yet be heard! We may not meet again but you are always in my heart. Farewell, Manaen, *the comforter*.' How long has it been? My own *abba* had explained the meaning of my name when I was young, on the cusp of manhood. I had tried to emulate my father through the years. He was a man of God—as is Nicodemus; I will miss him so! I turned from him before the tears began to flow.

Just then, Nicodemus said, 'Wait my friend, I have a surprise for you. Here is Nicolas; you remember that he became one of the "Serving Seven" in the early days of our sharing in the ministry. Nicolas is of the Diaspora—Antioch is his home. He is now returning to that city and it is his desire to escort you and Maryam if you would be willing to travel north with him.' 'Antioch? Of course! How wonderful. Nicolas, come with me now. Maryam and I will be so glad of your help!'

Nicolas picked up his luggage and came immediately with me and assisted with the final packaging of our necessities. I was glad that Maryam already knew our travelling companion. His presence would take from us much of the fear of an unknown future. Both Maryam and I were grieving the loss of David. Yet something of our son remained with us. It was his love for us, the memory of all he meant to us. Those final moments of his earthly life with us enabled a deep and abiding sense of joy and of *shalom* peace to rest within our soul. David had said, with his dying breath, 'The Nazarene is my Lord. I've found my faith, my Life… Yes, Lord, I am ready!' The grief is there but it mingles with a joy that cannot be passed by.

We were now to travel a new road. A new adventure awaited us, out there in the future. This would be "The Cross-bound Way". Its shadow invited us to reach out in faith to all that awaited us.

20. THE SEA ROUTE TO SYRIA

We managed to leave the city via the western gate before a guard was set against our exit. Thankfully, Nicolas had commandeered a donkey to be our beast of burden. The journey down through the mountains was tenuous but the sight of Joppa and the great Middle Sea filled us with relief though apprehension also mingled with our joy!

The Apostle Peter had supplied the address of a man by the name of Simon the Tanner, assuring us that we would be safe in his company. It rather amused me to think of Peter who had refused the eating of "unclean" food yet he had seen no problem in associating with a tanner of animal hides! Nor did we find a problem. We were so glad of Simon's hospitality. The conversation was certainly stimulating!

Time was short. We were aware that Herod's troops were intent on capturing us. We took ship hurriedly on the advice of Simon and scanned the shores of our beloved homeland. Would we see its soil, its almond blossom, again? A different springtime awaited us now.

Decisions had to be made as the ship neared Caesarea. Would we disembark to see the sights while the sailors concerned themselves with cargo and the like? No! We were advised to secret ourselves below deck and the wisdom of this option was seen through the portholes for there were troops scanning the movement of passengers. The captain was questioned. Being well paid for his discretion, the man held true to his word. He was believed. We were free now to travel into new territory, a land that had lain beyond our scant horizons.

The sea was kind to us. No storms impeded the journey. At times, no land could be discerned. We were "at sea" in more ways than one. But, in the main it was a pleasant experience. Our recent sorrows were lulled somewhat by the gentle lapping of the waves against the sturdy hull of the vessel as the wind in the sails took us northward. It was of interest to this land-dweller that a westerly wind could take a ship northward. The captain explained the phenomenon. 'It's the set of the sail, you see, not the force of the wind that truly

motivates a ship though the rudder may dictate a change of course!'
Our course was set. Strangely, we felt that we were not so much
running from a life-threatening situation as we were running to a
life-giving circumstance!

We were nearing Antioch. Beyond the western horizon—Italy
with its rampant empire—controlled the Mediterranean Sea. We were,
however, happily hugging the coast of Syria. We were in a "new world".
Could we cope with it? Left to our own devices, we were sure to fail.
With Holy Spirit "Wind" motivating our "sails" we will steer our "ship"
into the certainty that faith provides. All will be well. We knew it.

We carried our faith along with our luggage as we disembarked.
After thanking the captain and his crew for their kindness and safe-
keeping, we turned to meet up with more than the shore!!!

Impossible! Incredible! There was a man to meet us! Unbelievable! It was the "Terror from Tarsus"! The look of joyous recognition on his delighted face was more than I could comprehend. What's going on?

'Saul! Saul! You are the very last person I would have expected to see in Antioch! And, look at you, are you really you?!' A hearty laugh escaped from my erstwhile agitator. 'The brethren at Antioch requested that I come to meet you. We had been advised of your coming by a messenger sent from Jerusalem. Come, let us eat. We can catch up with all that's happened in the last few years. Maryam! You look so well. I must hear your news!'

We sat in a small public house that provided meals for transient travellers. 'Saul, there's been a dramatic change in you! The last time I saw you…' 'Yes, Manaen. Not a good look! I can never erase the memory of Stephen's demise in that wretched execution—for no wrong, just that he dared to believe the truth!'

'The truth, Saul? The truth? Do you believe it now? How is this possible?' 'Manaen, Maryam, Nicolas, I'm a new man! Me, a "Pharisee of the Pharisees"! It's not just that I changed my mind! I'm different in my soul! You ask how could it be? Well, I had been given official papers that provided me with the licence to persecute the Community of Faith in Damascus. You see, I'd done such a "good" job of it in Jerusalem, I was the very man who would cause the most havoc in the provinces!

'I was well on the way. It was early in the day when a light brighter than the sun—still in the east—shone on me from the north! 'What's this?' I thought. Then he spoke to me: "Saul, Saul, why are you persecuting me?" "Who are you? What do you mean?" "I am Jesus—the very person you are persecuting!" "But you are dead! How can this be?" Manaen, he took the time to explain and to counsel me! All my cohorts could attest later was to confirm the bright light and that I seemed to be talking to myself—though some extra sounds, possibly verbal, were discerned.

'I was advised to go on into the city of Damascus to seek out a man by the name of Ananias—he lives on Straight Street. Then, I was struck blind! Couldn't see a thing. That light had been much too bright. But now I think that the blindness was essential so that I could take the time to see with inner sight! Manaen! I saw the Light—in more ways than one. The truth had finally dawned on me.

When I turned up on Straight Street, I caused quite a stir. But Ananias had been instructed by the Lord to welcome me, settle me and introduce me to the local Christians—that's what we now call ourselves in Antioch! We are "the Church"—the fellowship you know as the Community of Faith!'

Nicolas was astounded, of course. He had been a member of the "Serving Seven" and had witnessed the stoning of his friend Stephen. How could he ever forgive this man? And yet, something was happening in his own soul. He also perceived this "new" Saul! Only the Lord can make changes in a person's life to match that which he saw in Saul.

'Saul,' he said, 'you were once in bondage to The Law. You haven't renounced The Law of God but it no longer has precedence in your life. The Law, for you, is now immersed in the free flow of the grace of God!' He did agree! And Maryam and I concurred!

'Come! It is time we were on our way to Antioch!' Our group, now so unified, at once began the short journey east. To our pleasant surprise, not only were we welcomed but, ah, the local *Christians* had secured adequate lodgings for us. We had "come home!"

The day had not concluded for me. I needed my writing kit! Many, many thoughts had crowded into my mind which needed to be said! Saul's testimony as to The Light drew forth this new psalm:

THE LIGHT OF THE WORLD
(Choir: *Hyfrydol* 8.7.8.7. D. Trochaic)

In a web of twisted ethics,
Many seek a path to tread,
Searching for a Light to guide them,
Needing to be safely led.
Light the world, Lord, souls are dying!
In the darkest realms of night
You still hold the Light of Heaven;
Saviour, lead us to this Light.

In a well of heartfelt sorrows,
Grievous pain invades the soul;
Where is hope for our tomorrows?
Where is help to make us whole?
Light this world, Lord, none decrying!
In the gloom of abject woe,
You will bring the Light of gladness;
Saviour, light our candle now!

In a waste of shattered precepts,
Maxims once held high have flown;
In the depths we search for meaning,
Where are virtues we could own?
Light Your world, Lord, Hell defying!
In the vales where shadows lay,
Lord, You are the Light we search for;
Saviour, be our Light today!

In this world where terror surges
And the nations rise in war,
Where's the peace plan, what's the answer
For our basic human flaw?

Light our world, Lord, none denying
On the road where grace will heal,
You will bear the torch of freedom;
Saviour, now Your Light reveal!

Next day, we were able to sit in conference with *The Church*, (I liked the term and more so, the name: *Christian*–this, indeed, was a name most meaningful. I was sure that both terms would stay with us, always!

Glad greetings were shared all round. I was more than pleased to discover that there were, already in the group, some whom I had met previously. There was the young man known as John Mark—I was sure that he would make his "mark" upon the Church! And there was a person whom I knew as Joseph but referred to here as Barnabas. What a man of grace he is. I understand that he and John Mark are related. To my mind, they were related in two ways: by reason of family ties and also, they were brothers in the Faith! And Maryam and I were so pleased to find ourselves included in the Church "family" at Antioch!

Maryam and I will be glad to give our heart and hands to the task of sharing our faith and leading people to know the Christ! Already, I am finding that the Greek language is not so alien to me now. I will be able to converse adequately with the people of Antioch.

We were learning new ways in which to be good shepherds of the "flock" of God. And I learned something more: as I reflected on the advance of the Gospel into new territory, I realised that this was of the Lord. And now, a new discernment came upon my soul. I had thought of *Yeshua*, Jesus, as the *kebes*—Lamb of God—who would take the sins of the world upon himself so that there could be an AT-ONE-MENT, a reconciliation between *YHVH* and humankind. I see at last that my Friend—*the Lamb*—is actually *The Shepherd, THE GOOD SHEPHERD WHO GAVE HIS LIFE FOR THE SHEEP!*

This realisation is bringing a deeper spiritual maturity to me! Not only is Jesus *the Lamb of God* who reconciled me unto *YHVH El Shaddai*, He is *the Good Shepherd* who daily nurtures my soul, settles me in green pastures; He leads me by quiet waters; He steers me in righteous paths; He cares for me in life's shadowed vales; His guiding staff and guarding rod comfort me; He restores my soul; I have all I need; goodness and mercy attend me all my life; and He will bring me Home to His Fold! And what a fold this is!

21. REFLECTIONS

My beloved princess *Mimi* and I were immersed immediately in the ministries of the Church at Antioch. We are becoming Christians not only by designation but by action! My role fell upon natural lines for I became the resident rabbi! That is, I am the elder statesman teacher of those new-born into The Faith. I daily open to view the heritage of the past and how the ancient truths revealed the coming of the *Mashiach*— the Messiah, Christ, the Anointed One: the *kebes* Lamb of God who is the Good Shepherd that gave His life to redeem humankind.

Before I sign off for the night, it seems appropriate to reflect upon all the events, the experiences, that have led us to this new life which is showering us with such abundant blessings. There are people in this Community of Faith who are already gifting us with a sense of family, a sense of belonging, of well-being. There is love in this place, there is grace, there is peace. And I realise the reason for it all. I found that reason, first, in a fetid, straw littered stable. All this has set me thinking. The writing kit will assist me as I reflect on a journey like no other:

LUCILLE L. TURFREY

ON THE ROAD

It was a rocky road to Bethlehem!
The precious parchments of the Patriarchs
had set the scene on history's holy page.
The sacred signs were there. Messiah's Day
would dawn when God's own time had fully come.
A star proclaimed The Hour and angels sang
'Good news! The Peasant Prince is birthed in straw.'

It was a winding way to Nazareth!
A village youth, at work among the shavings of
the shop where wooden things were hewn, once paused
to stretch his arms as shafts of light etched out
his silhouette upon the waiting wall.
The shadowed shape traced not a carpenter
But victim, cast upon a cross of shame!

It was a pleasant path by Galilee!
The rabbi from obscurity strode down
the dusty road beside that sea so prone
to trouble workers on the wave. He marched
into the mart where wondrous words would hold
the throng enthralled and grasping for God's News,
the Gospel of a Kingdom near at hand.

It was a craggy course, discipleship!
He called his own, as rabbis do, out from
the ordinary and bland, the fishing and
the taxing, too. He moulded, melded them
and minded them to down their nets, take up
their cross to follow him. No turning back,
no wavering on the way ahead of them.

ON THE ROAD — Continued

It was a torturous trail, throughout this land
where, steadfastly, he strode toward his goal.
His wisdom at a village well brought peace
to one so wrong and wronged. He offered draughts
of living water, quenching all soul thirst.
The blind, the lame, the lepers, wasted ones
found hope and wholeness in his healing touch.

They were such stately streets, Jerusalem's.
Downtrodden by the alien force of Rome,
the city also suffered men so holy to
themselves but far from God in Temple veils.
His challenge to the blasphemies, the sins,
injustices of priests and king, would take
him to a cross, the rugged frame of death.

It was a treacherous track to Calvary!
The shouldered beam, the bloodied back bent low
from lashings cruelly cast, the thorny crown,
the pains much deeper than a soldier's spear he knew.
He bore our griefs and deepest pain of sin and laid
them in the tomb of God's forgetfulness,
those sins of ours, releasing us to life!

It was a radiant road of joy from out
the empty tomb so near that knoll,
Golgotha's ghastly face, that 'Calvary'.
The resurrection dawn extends its glow
upon this precious path. So where, O death,
is now your sting, your conquering, gaping grave?
The victory is Christ's, the Lord of Life!

Printed in Australia
AUHW020559200721
348936AU00001B/2